HESSMAN'S
NECKLACE

ADVANCE PRAISE FOR

HESSMAN'S NECKLACE

"An excellent analyst of noir writing, Nicholas Litchfield has now written a terrific mystery novel of his own. *Hessman's Necklace* combines the impeccable plotting of *The Maltese Falcon* with the canny post-modernism of *Chinatown*. In it, a flawed ladies' man, an enigmatic beauty, and an acquisitive man of the cloth join a hunt for an artifact that exposes fault lines of corruption and perversion in 1950s America. Suspenseful, savvy and self-referential, Nicholas Litchfield's *Hessman's Necklace* soon will be added to the canon of enduring noir novels."
—LAURENCE KLAVAN, Edgar Award winner, librettist of *Bed and Sofa*

"Ray Stokes walks the meanest streets of noir territory in Nicholas Litchfield's *Hessman's Necklace*. But those streets soon become a cursed, corrupt path as he is sent by his boss to steal a valuable necklace. It should be a simple assignment, but when Stokes encounters it around the neck of a woman as hard as the diamonds themselves, his descent into darkness truly begins. A cracking great read!"
—JAMES R. BENN, author of A Billy Boyle WWII Mystery Series

"Ray Stokes is a Chicago fixer, a heavy drinker and a despicable playboy. He takes what he wants and who he wants. But when his criminal boss sends him to South Boston to steal a priceless stolen necklace, the beautiful woman wearing it is more than he can handle. Nicholas Litchfield brings his noir characters to life with Chandleresque dialogue and Dashiell Hammett twists. A fun, fast, five-star read."
—MICKEY J. CORRIGAN, author of *What I Did for Love* and *Project XX*

"A wealthy collector sends his amoral gofer to Boston to steal a diamond necklace from a corrupt reverend. The plan: seduce the reverend's girlfriend and take the necklace. Crackling dialogue and a depraved cast of characters make this a noir thriller you can't put down."
—ART BELL, author of *What She's Hiding*

"*Hessman's Necklace* is an engaging romp through a time of stylish noir, the late 1950s, an era of wise guys, whiskey, and wild women all tangled up in crimes that often turn violent. The cars are fast, the talk is tough, the guns blaze. Nicholas Litchfield lovingly recreates an atmosphere in which tough guy Ray Stokes, jaded crook and cocky ladies man, gets more than he bargained for. He is out on the road, on the hunt for a valuable necklace last seen around the neck of a beautiful woman. Will he get what he's after? Meantime, what—or who—is after him? This gripping story is well worth the read."

—MARK JACOBS, author of *A Handful of Kings* and *Stone Cowboy*

"*Hessman's Necklace* is a fast-paced enjoyable read. I pictured the anti-hero Ray as what a young Philip Marlowe might have been like, if Marlowe was hungover, had fewer moral scruples, and had turned his skills to crime instead of detective work. We can't really approve of his behavior, but because Ray's target is other even-more hardened criminals, we urge him onward as he narrowly avoids one disastrous situation after another. Like Marlowe, he takes punches, literally and figuratively, and keeps on getting up, and we root for his luck to hold. Danger is never far away, and there are taut scenes of violence and impending violence. An America, not so far in the distant past, but culturally distinct from today, is evoked in gritty streets, diners, and seedy motels. I won't give it away here, but trust me, the ending is fraught with suspense and surprises."

—ROBERT GARNER McBREARTY, author of *A Night at the Y* and *The Problem You Have*

HESSMAN'S NECKLACE

— A Novel —

NICHOLAS LITCHFIELD

Lowestoft
Chronicle
Press

LCP

Copyright © 2025 by Nicholas Litchfield

First edition: June 2025

Cover and book design by Nicholas Litchfield
Art credits include: iStock/CSA-Printstock

Print edition ISBN-13: 978-1-7323328-5-0

Library of Congress Control Number: 2024951036

Printed and bound in the United States of America

For Arthur and Ava, who make the day better whenever they show up

HESSMAN'S
NECKLACE

One

Ray Stokes peeled off his sweat-soaked banana-colored shirt, pulled it over his head without removing the buttons, and tossed it onto the back of the drab accent chair beside the writing bureau. There was a roguish look in his russet brown eyes, a twinkle of mischief in his bearing that hinted he would be an inconsiderate nuisance. There was sweetness and passion in him, but his brazen impudence usually got in the way of any virtuous qualities.

"Does this whet your appetite?" he asked the woman sprawled across the kitschy floral comforter on his king-size mattress whose lovely cobalt blue eyes bore into him, greedily probing every inch of his sinewy, tan body.

His smooth, masculine voice flaunted confidence and charm, and the way he stuck out his chest, practically demanding her to express words of glowing admiration for what lurked beneath the garments, was slightly irritating. The woman said nothing, and her thin, unsmiling lips divulged little, but her fixated stare laid bare what was on her mind. To a gourmand, he was as tantalizing as a superior Baked Alaska exhibiting a sublime igloo of browned meringue, and the way she surveyed him intimated she was positively ravenous.

He moved toward her, relishing the indecent glint in her sultry eyes. The unmistakable concentration on her face made his ego bloat. It was not an uncommon sight—the famine. That pained craving engraved in a woman's expression during foreplay; the need to touch his firm, bronzed skin, imbibe the taste of his manly sweat. His aphrodisiacal scent was often too much to bear for those of a voracious disposition, and he could tell without needing to inquire that the very nearness of him made this woman moist with desire.

As he climbed onto the bed, the beleaguered huddle of neglected fleshiness murmured with patent exhilaration. They were garbled noises posing as words, sentiments that were as devoid of value as charred old meat. Ray's fingers enveloped her enormous bosoms, which were arguably her best features. She was soft and chubby and twitching with anticipation; there was a tiny bead of sweat on her temple, betraying the sweltering fervor she felt for him. Her frantic mood signaled she wouldn't be able to hold out much longer, and he was seized by a sudden mischievous desire to prolong her agony.

She gave him an incredulous look as he broke away from her and reached for the bottle of liquor on the bedside table. It was a Glenfiddich Special single malt whisky in a curvaceous container, the red lettering on the label emphasizing the word *special*. Heck, it certainly was singularly good, he thought, admiring the shapely bottle. He took a long, greedy swig and then sighed contentedly. The citrus and oaky sugars and baked fruit flavors came in waves, making his throat tingle blissfully. It was the best beverage he had quaffed in hours, days, perhaps weeks. The gulp he had taken was divine, delivering a sensation that loitered in his mouth. The taste persuaded him that the thirst-quencher was maybe better than Glenlivet, a joyful concoction of silky, vanilla sweetness, or Macallan, or Jack Daniel's Tennessee Whiskey. Ray handled the bottle affectionately, wishing it wasn't his only one. Like the best things in life, his firewater brought him elation and disruptiveness and then evaporated from his life, leaving disappointment and suffering.

"I'm not enough for you?" she griped. "You need Dutch

courage to take me on?"

He grinned crookedly. "That what you think, darling? Give over. You're more than enough. More than any man might want. My throat was parched, that's all."

"I'm what?" she said, glowering. "I'm *more* than you want. Is that what you're saying? What is that? Code for too fat? I'm excessive, overmuch? What d'you mean exactly?"

He chose not to allay her qualms and, instead, gave a contrite shrug of his broad shoulders, muttering inarticulately, adhering to the guiding principle that it was always best to leave a woman insecure and eager to please and gratify the whims of her man. Then he took another gluttonous slug of the whisky, leaving only meager dregs in the bottle. He wanted to drain it completely, but he also couldn't bear the idea that there wouldn't be a single drop of alcohol left in his home. There was sadness in an empty container, a pleasure removed, its value expunged.

He set the container back on the table with a resounding thump, unconcerned about leaving a disfiguring mark on the surface. It was an elegant Italian mid-century bedside table, a beautiful piece of Mahogany furniture, perhaps the highlight of the room. Ray didn't much care for it despite its apparent splendor. He didn't care much for any of his possessions, even though he had paid a decent amount of cash to lavishly furnish his home. Though he loved money, he was still figuring out the most rewarding way to spend it.

The woman scowled at him but quickly forgot the affront when he returned his lips to her neck. They were thin, stingy lips and rather inadequate compared to the rest of him, and yet they clamped down on her like suction cups, and for the next hour, he savored her voluptuous body and devoted himself to satisfying her insatiable lust.

It was a torturous night where he thought his heart might give out on him. Despite being in his twenties—for one more year, at any rate—his nightly routine impacted his stamina. Excessive liquor consumption and a disinclination to allow a day of rest into his hectic social calendar did him no favors. Still, he rejected the idea of taking a night off. He had earned the nickname "The Reveler," and he was proud of the moniker and keen to maintain the party-hard profile in the community. His typical schedule after sundown was something to marvel at: Dinner at Trousseau's, cocktails at the Truman Club, dancing at LaSalle's, followed by more drinks and a flutter at some of the shady betting stalls in the newest pop-up gin bars, and then, time and again, a senseless brawl in one of the dark alleyways near The Crooked Copper. Sometimes, he liked to cap the evening off with a few bawdy songs and a hookah pipe at Madam Carousel. Often, his nights went on and on with no end in sight, and they were consumed with revelry. Occasionally, work got in the way. Otherwise, he poured his heart and soul into having a good time. Try as he might, he couldn't remember the last time he had settled for a quiet night with a book.

Tonight, he had brought the merrymaking out of the clubs and to his home, and though he was well aware of what sort of lady he had lured back to his bedroom, he had misjudged her. She was an untamed tigress, full of desire and devilry. Initially, he was thrilled with her and enthusiastic to bestow compliments… for the first couple of hours. There was a moment when his eyes explored with great affection the contours of her face, glossing over the manifest creases and pockmarks and stray hairs and finding something to cherish about her large, full lips, flourishing eyebrows, and even her prominent nose. Her adorably feverish demeanor and the ugly, garroted sounds that emanated from her told him she was having a thoroughly wonderful time and probably deemed him an estimable lover.

Unsurprisingly, his ardor dissipated, inch by inch, as the evening wore on. All the same, his verdict was that it had been an evening well spent and a night to remember. At least, he hoped he would remember it. Eventually, the allure would drain out of her, and by sunrise, she would have overstayed her welcome. Ray had no time for clingy women. For him, intimacy was confined to the bedroom, and the mornings tended to be sobering affairs. He knew very little about his latest conquest and intended to keep it that way.

Fortunately for him, the woman had a similar mindset, and he was simply a means to an end. Regrettably, she wasn't as tolerant and easily placated as Ray had hoped. Several times, he bit down hard on the feather pillow, his teeth almost tearing through the pillowcase. The excellent booze did nothing to suppress the pain she was causing him. She was a vile, feral beast, undeserving of his divine, sculpted body, and he buried his face in the pillow, trying not to swear out loud, resisting the urge to beg for mercy. The way she dug her sharp nails into his back, drawing blood, and beat her fists on his backside, imploring him to work harder, was almost too much to handle. He whimpered and grappled with her squirming bulk, anxious to be free. The way her thighs trapped him made escape impossible, and he found himself muttering, "God help me! You're killing me!"

Though he began to despise her and yearned to be elsewhere, his longing for a reprieve didn't last long. Pleasure eventually overcame pain, as it always did. Truth be told, her horridly rough behavior added interesting savagery to the night's excitement.

Disconcertingly, as the overlong evening jollity wore on, his surroundings became a blur, and a chill permeated the room. The hammering in his chest became almost too much to endure, and his rhythmic gyrations came to a clumsy halt. He clutched the top rail of the metal bedpost tightly, unable to draw another breath. It was as if someone had shut off his oxygen supply, and he was now mutely pleading for air and fearful of the strain on his heart. It was a tense, frightening moment. Again, he had disregarded the warnings and found himself beyond safe margins.

Then his ears suddenly popped—the silence broken by delirious moans and the headboard banging against the wall.

With frantic relief, he caught his breath, the tightness in his chest rapidly subsiding. Immediately, he rolled over and lay on his back, panting, grateful that the excruciating mêlée was over. Although sore and worried about his health, he was proud of his accomplishments and buoyed by a sense of fulfillment.

Swiftly, his eyelids became heavy, and he lost the battle to stay awake. Alas, he was denied a peaceful entrance to the land of nod. Minutes into his well-earned rest, he was jolted back to consciousness by his new lover's tremendous fidgeting. The bedspring squawked, and she refused to keep still.

"Pull yourself together, mister," she growled, throwing herself on top of him with undue roughness. "The night isn't over yet. I came here for action."

The warning brought a taut, panicky stirring in his chest, and he found himself short of breath once more and suffering a fiery pain in his loins.

"I came home with you expecting something more. There was the look of a bullfighter about you—a dynamism that vowed to tease and exhaust and ultimately conquer whatever you came up against. I thought you'd be a man experienced in seduction techniques, a man who could make a woman giddy with desire." She waggled her index finger at him in a threatening manner and hissed, "Don't you dare disappoint me. I won't abide a milksop between the sheets."

Ray winced perceptibly, wishing for an immediate escape. Their bodies were entwined to the point that he felt acutely trapped. The usually passionate man gazed deeply into her willful eyes, wondering why they held no appeal. A sumptuous, picture-perfect creature was urging him to greater sensual heights, yet he was utterly bereft of carnal yearning. He tried to purge all evidence of revulsion from his contorted face. It was no easy feat. The more he gazed at her, the more he felt his mouth prickling with aversion. She looked hideously mean and selfish and full of gluttony. He used the strength he had left in him to shove her off his fatigued body.

She squealed with shock. The boorish way he pushed her away sealed his fate.

"*Selfish rake*," she raged. "You sad excuse for a lover. A howler monkey has more going on between his thighs. How dare you ruin this for me!"

The violence in her tone was otherworldly, and it was grim work listening to her venomous coil of resentment.

"You're nothing but a damn eunuch. The hell was I thinking coming back here with you?" Her pointed, horny nails seemed to expand, the malevolent digits looking like claws. "What's the value in having male anatomy if you don't know how to use it?"

He felt an urgency to get back into his clothes, alarmed at the way her horrid-looking fingernails clawed at the sheets. They were nails ready to do damage, prepared to vandalize what didn't belong to her.

He felt an awkward jolt in his groin as his testicles retracted into his body. The woman had managed to drive all semblance of lust out of him, and the scratching sound of those frightening nails tearing up the bedsheets warned him that right now, he was easy prey.

I've got to go, he tried to say, but the words didn't want to be heard. Her umbrage told him to say little—better yet, say nothing at all. With luck, he could make it out of the bed and into his clothes before she realized his intentions.

"What do you have to say for yourself?" she continued. "What's your excuse for that crummy performance?"

He couldn't offer a coherent reply. Actually, right then, he found it difficult to think rationally without his underwear, so he sprang out of bed and gathered his things from the floor with the keenness of a man who had just heard the barman cry, "Last call!"

"That gorgeous body is pointless titillation. You're just a coward and a bore," she ranted while he pulled up his briefs.

His baggy, gabardine slacks caused him some bother, and he

stumbled as he got his left foot through the wide pant leg.

The fresh creak of the bedsprings told him she had also gotten out of the bed, but he didn't dare turn to look at her, sensing an irrevocable hatred toward him. He decided to keep his cruel mouth shut and focus on getting his pants buttoned, pulling on his clothes faster than at any other time. He intended to kick her out of his home once he had laced his shoes. Yet, there was some gallantry left in him—he would give her some money and guide her toward the nearest phone booth so she could call a cab.

As he grabbed his shirt from the chair and ineptly tried to get one arm into the sleeve, he sensed she was standing directly behind him. There was an icy chill in the air, and at once, he was filled with dread. He whirled around in time to meet the full force of the bottle of Scotch in her hand as it struck him solidly across the side of his face.

As the remaining dregs of liquid in the bottle flew across the room, Ray dropped gracelessly to the floor without uttering a sound, and to the girl's satisfaction, he sank into immediate unconsciousness.

━━ ✦ ━━

The obstinate chime of the telephone forced Ray out of his bedroom and into the hallway of his tastefully designed yet diminutive home. His limbs were heavy and the three-pound organ taking up precious space in his cranium was not functioning as it should. Twice, he bumped into things that were not in his direct path. The 19th-century English clock, which he banged into with his hip, hurt the most. It was a tall case clock with decorative brass ball finials and a carved split-pediment top. It had detailed vine and leaf carvings and a colorful painted surround that illustrated a tavern scene from *Tam o' Shanter*, the wonderful narrative poem written by the Scottish poet Robert Burns in 1790. Ray's boss, Walter Cartwell, had recommended it to him, having seen it advertised by a local dealer he was familiar with, and he practically insisted Ray buy it. Lovely though it was, that type of luxurious room-filler was hardly Ray's style. He preferred modern things, and this was excessive and unnecessary. The large, heavy object represented big money he could have frittered away at the racetrack or spent at one of his many drinking holes.

As Ray neared the telephone, its shrill tone sent agonizing jolts to his brain. He broke into a pathetic jog, hurrying to reach the receiver and end its reign of terror.

"Ray, I need you over here now."

It was Walter, and he sounded more desperate than usual.

Ray curled his lip, wishing it had been somebody else. Work was the last thing he wanted to contemplate right then.

"I'm not feeling so well," confided Ray. "I'm as weak as a kitten. I think I need a day to rest and recuperate."

"There's no time for that. I need you here now."

Ray tapped the receiver against his chin, taking a moment to think up a sound excuse. Nothing suitable swooped through his thoughts. "I'm having car trouble," he lamely said. "Can it wait until later in the day?"

"I'll send a car over to pick you up."

"No, there's no need for that."

"Be ready in ten minutes," Walter advised.

"Wait. Hold on a minute."

He was feeling faint. Ten minutes wasn't nearly enough time to get himself together. He could scarcely see straight, and quite what Walter would make of him when he staggered into the old man's home didn't bear thinking about.

"I need to dress and shave and grab some coffee. I can't leave here just yet. Will one o'clock be okay?"

"One o'clock will *not* be okay."

The anger in the man's voice was unsettling. It was never wise to say or do something that would upset Walter Cartwell. He was a man who made excessive demands, and he expected a great deal from people, especially those who served him. Let Walter down at your peril; he wasn't the forgiving type.

"That job you did for me in San Fran last April. You remember the cufflinks?"

"Cool blue fireworks bursting in the night sky."

"I like your description. They had those striking blue guilloche enamels set in gold. The engraving beneath the enamels gave the appearance of blue fireworks."

"They were exquisite. Worth the time and sweat it took to get them."

"You think?"

"Well, weren't they?" said Ray, slightly confused.

"I never told you the entire story, did I? My bad."

Ray leaned against the wall, rubbing his eyes. He wanted to hear the story, but he wanted to go back to bed more.

"Kent Malone attempted to get the cufflinks about six months before you did. He broke into Cristiano Puiggarí's home thinking he hadn't been detected, but he must have set off a silent alarm. Cristiano's watchman cornered him in one of the upstairs bedrooms and beat him to a pulp. The police were never called, and Kent was never seen again."

"Did somebody talk? How did you hear what happened to him?"

"His left hand was delivered to my home. A 14-karat yellow gold ring was still attached to the middle finger. It was an Egyptian Pharoah signet ring. Looked rather splendid."

"Jesus!"

"The ring was worth quite a bit of money, but they left it on his finger so I could identify the victim. They knew he worked for me. Poor Kent."

Ray was sickened by the news. He hadn't known Kent Malone well, and he had only met him on a couple of occasions, but the revelation made his stomach turn.

"Why didn't you tell me this six months ago?"

"Why do you think? I figured you probably wouldn't take the job if you learned what happened to Kent."

There was no "probably" about it. Ray absolutely would not have taken the job.

"You let me break into Cristiano Puiggarí's home only six months after he'd caught a thief in one of his bedrooms?"

"That's right. I knew I could count on you. I highly doubt there's anybody better in the whole darn country."

The praise failed to gratify him. "And now you want me to do another job? Something perilous and fraught with difficulty, no doubt?"

"That's right."

He felt the urge to put the telephone receiver back in the cradle. "I'd like to take some time off," he flatly told his employer. "I want to travel a little. Take in a few counties, see some sights. I think a three-month tour of Europe might do me the world of good."

"In my opinion, I don't think it would. I need you on this next job, Ray. You've not disappointed me yet, and I don't believe you will this time, either."

"Listen, Walter…"

The old man wouldn't let him finish. "It's double pay."

An excited chill went through Ray. "Double, you say?"

"Yes, double. Now, get over here as fast as you can. I need you here within the hour."

Walter rang off. He had said all he needed to say.

Two

The loud, rumbling sound of the Chevrolet Corvette disturbed the peaceful woodland scenery as Ray made his way down the twisty private road to Walter Cartwell's lavish country home. His convertible's smooth, beautiful curves camouflaged what was, otherwise, a raspy, underwhelming vehicle colored in eye-popping Pennant Blue. Although it had a tasteful beige interior, it was dressed in a poor-quality fiberglass plastic body and leaked like a sieve. Not even a slicker could keep Ray dry on the freeway on a rainy day.

The car sped across Walter's expansive stone gravel driveway, making the clean stone snarl as the tires locked and the Corvette skidded to a jerky halt near the front entrance. A plume of dense black dust wafted past the sprawling front porch and across the large lawn, settling into the artistically pruned bushes.

Ray cut the engine and tossed his expensive sunglasses onto the dashboard. He opened the driver's door and flopped his left leg out of the vehicle. The heel of his Italian woven leather loafer crunched down onto the machine-crushed stone, and instantly, he retracted his foot, returning it to the floor of the car. Concerned about his appearance, he shifted slightly in his seat and peered warily at his reflection in the interior mirror. The ashen face that stared back at him filled him with dismay.

He put a hand to his head and tugged at his forelocks. The wind had played havoc with his medium-length auburn hair.

After smoothing down the tufts at the sides and sweeping the tousled top back into a plump pompadour, he dug his fingernails into his scalp with bitterness, but the pain hardly registered.

He felt shriveled and empty and more like an old man rather than the youthful, full-of-ambition gadabout everyone perceived him to be. His bloodshot eyes gave everyone a good idea of the hedonistic lifestyle he led. The previous night, after a vivacious time with the Chicago Cardinals, causing a stir at his various clubs, he had been up until dawn getting to grips with a good bottle of Scotch and a badly behaved office secretary. Both had nearly killed him. When he woke that morning, his body felt like the wrestler Lou Thesz had just attempted a variation of his powerbomb move, twirling him in the air until he was so dizzy he couldn't tell the difference between the ceiling and the floor, then cartwheeling him down onto the mat on his neck and shoulders.

Ray took a deep breath and looked disgustedly at the ugly bruise on his cheek exacted by the hot-tempered dame with an unquenchable sex drive. He found out too late that she derived pleasure from pain—chiefly his. Any slither of affection he felt toward her had burned to ashes. Somehow, his cheekbone was still intact.

After adjusting the collar of his jacket and straightening his purple rayon hand-painted leaf tie, he got out of the vehicle. The car was pristine, unscratched; there were no perceptible dents or discolorations, nothing to indicate it had been mishandled. Ray was not the gentle type, however, and he lived in the moment, rarely concerning himself with defacing his belongings. The car would bruise and leak and corrode. That was inevitable. It might not last for long, and that was fine with him. As with lovers, when imperfections became clear, he looked for a replacement rather than attempting to fix a problem.

Ray kicked at the door and heard it slam shut. Then he lumbered across the driveway, his shoes making slight grooves in the crushed rock. As he staggered up the steps to Walter's front door, using a porch column for support, he tried his best to ignore the dull throb in his head. Four cups of rancid motor oil posing as coffee had gotten him out of his home, but the liquid jiggling about in his stomach made him feel sure it would come back up at some point during the day—maybe even on his boss' carpet.

He rapped on the door, and the bronze door knocker sent an unpleasant vibration up his arm, causing his gums to hurt. While he waited on the porch of the grand residence, trying to focus his attention on anything but the advancing ache behind his eyes, he examined the aged Victorian knocker. It was a child's hand, puny and blemished. Though its age eluded him, it was clearly an ancient adornment. According to Walter, these types of knockers were thought to originate from the hamsa, also known as the hand of Fatima. It was a palm-shaped amulet, common throughout North Africa and the Middle East, used to protect against evil. The knocker looked more ghoulish than quaint, and right then, it wasn't proving effective.

He was about to have another go with it, but the possibility that he might cause damage held him back. It may have lasted decades unscathed, but that didn't mean it was impervious to his clumsiness.

He placed his forehead against the solid door to cool his skin, deciding to give up on the knocker. This was the second time he had visited Walter's home in a week. The last job, which had taken him to Washington, D.C., for two days to pick up a 13th-century *tanto* sword from a historian's private collection, had been brought to such a swift, successful conclusion that it had earned him a sizable bonus. No prints, no witnesses, no call for violence. Ray wished all assignments could be so clean and trouble-free. The one disappointment had been the loss of his lock picks. The mystery of where he had left them had put him in a state of panic. It was the sort of glaring mistake that was best not to dwell on, especially considering the possible ramifications should the picks be traced back to him.

Ray knew little about his new assignment other than that it excited his unemotional boss. In their telephone conversation an hour earlier, the humorless old man had been unexpectedly lively and talkative, although his revelation about poor Kent Malone didn't sit well with Ray. It was a reminder that he was disposable, his life worth no more than a pair of exclusive cufflinks.

It was a mistake coming to Walter's residence; he was sure of it. The man's insistence on him coming as soon as possible revealed that time wasn't on his side. Big money was on the table, and the expectations were higher than ever. In the five years Ray had known Walter, he had never seen him act this way, and while he welcomed the fat paycheck, he was apprehensive about the job. Walter would only offer such a large sum if it was perilous and there was a surfeit of willing candidates.

When the front door finally swung open, a heavy-set man with a pockmarked face and a horrid purple scar on his left cheek emerged. Thick tufts of hair protruded from his broad, misshaped nose, and his small, beady eyes were set in deep hollows. The eyes were of such a dark brown shade that they appeared black.

Ray was familiar with all of Walter's lackeys, and Günter, a relatively new recruit, was an exceptionally revolting member of Walter's household. His jagged teeth and twisted features gave him the appearance of a much-abused boxer. He was uncouth, insolent, and aggressive. Disconcertingly, he was remarkably articulate and adept at delivering a quick, low blow to one's ego.

At the sight of Ray, his thin lips curled in dissatisfaction. "Oh, it's you," he said in his deep, accented voice.

"Who did you expect?"

"Somebody interesting."

Günter's welcome made Ray feel as appetizing as discovering pubic hair in one's half-eaten sandwich. "Walter didn't mention that I was on my way over?"

Günter shrugged. "He may have mentioned it. A lot has happened this morning."

"Like what? Is there something I should know?"

"There's nothing you need to know," said Günter coldly.

"Let me be the judge of that. Has there been a lot of foot traffic here already? Anyone else show up before me?"

"That's really none of your business. Is it?"

Ray managed to keep his temper under control, though it certainly wasn't easy. Günter appeared to be an expert at being insolent and nasty, and he could get under Ray's skin in a matter of seconds. It was scary to think what he might achieve if they spent a full hour in one another's company.

"What's put you in such a good mood, anyway?"

"I seem bothered?" said Günter.

"You seem especially bothered. You're behaving like a jilted husband," said Ray, hoping the vicious secretary he had spent the night with might be Günter's wife.

"There's an aura about you that I don't like, Ray," admitted Günter. "It antagonizes me. I feel a compunction to sock you in the mouth."

The glint in his eyes warned Ray to be on guard.

"Perhaps a jab to the stomach and an uppercut to the chin. Then a right hook to your nose, like a hammer blow, while you're falling backward," he added.

Ray pictured the boxing combinations and felt slightly winded by Günter's imagined flurry of punches.

"I don't know you well—probably a good thing—but you have that infuriating expression whenever you come here. A supercilious look. Makes me yearn to wipe it off your face. Bash it until it's a bloody pulp."

"Don't hold back, will you," Ray said, trying to make light of the unpleasant remarks. "It's good to know how a man feels about his colleague."

"I'm blessed with two good fists," Günter said proudly. "And I'm tempted to belt you the way your father should have belted you when you were a little boy."

"I was never that little," Ray said coolly.

"No? I imagine you were rude and obnoxious, though. Deserving of a beating but spared one. It wouldn't take much to knock you down, Ray. You're a weak-minded wimp who's pretending to be tough. But you don't fool me. Your knuckles look as fragile as baby teeth, and I bet your skin is paper-thin. A whack to your cheek with a folded newspaper would split you open like an overripe tomato. You would gush blood everywhere and probably make a mess of my shirt. I doubt I could hold back once I started on you. I might keep slamming these iron-like knuckles into your childish face until the bones and cartilage snap and the cartoonish Papier-mâché head you love so much is no longer recognizable."

He paused, enjoying the appalled expression on Ray's face. Then he added casually, "You must get that a lot, *ja*? *Du bist eine Kakerlake, die getötet werden muss.*"

As Ray didn't speak German, the words were lost on him. It was probably a good thing, as he doubted Günter was capable of offering compliments.

Again, he used humor to counter the man's vicious remarks, saying, "I usually only have that effect on bookies or the occasional office secretary. As for mangled faces, yours is the sort only a mother could love. But I'm sure you're the exception. I can't imagine she dared look at it often."

"Get inside the house," Günter responded snappily.

His patience had now abandoned him entirely. There was a pinkness in his face, a fiery glow brightening the purple scar on his left cheek. His hands also seemed to be trembling, though it was not because of fear but because of excitement. They were pulsating with gusto, energized by the prospect of pummeling Ray's fine-looking face into a distinctly different shape.

"Worst manservant ever," grumbled Ray, stepping into the house, unconscious of the menace his colleague posed.

He took his eyes off Günter to admire the plush burgundy

carpet. It was new and tasteful and in keeping with the rest of the elegant decor.

"I'm not the butler," growled Günter, giving Ray a little shove in the chest.

Ray had to grab hold of the corner of the front door to avoid tumbling backward. His eyes showed fury as he watched Günter retreat down the elongated, wood-paneled hallway, muttering crossly in German. The raspy words were grotesque. Ray kicked the door shut angrily and followed the man through the house, fantasizing about hitting him in the back of the head with the butt of his revolver.

Günter stopped at the handsome oak door to Walter's study. He took a moment to clear his throat, then rapped loudly on the wood with his powerful knuckles. "Stokes is here," he announced, almost shouting the words.

There was no response, so he thumped his fist against the door.

"Yes, okay," said Walter, absently.

Günter muttered in a low voice, "Incidentally, you need a bath, Stokes. You stink."

He opened the door and brusquely signaled to Ray to go inside.

"Makes an entertaining change to hear the domestics chastise their superiors, doesn't it?" Ray sneered.

Günter's face twitched with annoyance. "You're not my superior."

Ray wouldn't accept it. The man was of inferior stock and most definitely beneath him.

"Any normal guy burdened with a hideous face like yours would do the decent thing and blow his goddamn brains out," whispered Ray.

He was too slow to evade Günter's fast hands, and there was a sharp, painful tug at his neck as the aggressive thug grabbed Ray's purple rayon tie. He drew Ray's face close to his, and for a prickly moment, Ray thought the man was about to deliver a Scottish kiss. His nose had not yet been broken, and he was sure that the power in Günter's headbutt would split his head open like a piñata.

Ray somehow managed to pry his tie free and push the tough guy away. In a quiet, albeit seething tone, he said, "You'll regret doing that."

Then he pushed hotly past Günter and strode assertively into Walter's large yet cluttered study.

Three

The aged man was hunched over his desk, carefully inspecting a pair of very old spectacles. He didn't look up.

As Günter slammed the door closed and retreated down the hallway, Ray padded across the room, appreciating the Bessarabian rugs and the stained-glass doors and pine paneling throughout. He glanced around at the many exquisite pieces of antique furniture and fascinating little china and marble objects in display cabinets. Baroque paintings were on the walls; a grandiose Rubens reproduction caught his eye. Every time he entered Walter's gorgeous home, he discovered exquisite objects he hadn't previously observed.

"Take a seat," said Walter, aware of Ray's shadow looming over him.

Ray spilled into the seat by Walter's desk, relieved to be off his feet again. He looked with mild curiosity at the spectacles in his boss' hands. They had no ear loops, and the green lenses gave them the appearance of novelty glasses.

"You got here remarkably quickly," said Walter, approvingly, looking at Ray for the first time.

"Yes, the roads were quiet, and my car—noisy gas-guzzler that it is—takes the bends awfully nicely."

"You really shouldn't drive so fast. You'll attract the wrong kind of attention," Walter chided. He peered hard at Ray, noticing his bloodshot eyes and the dark blotch on his cheek.

"It's nothing," volunteered Ray. "I caught my face on a beam in the basement last night while trying to reset the breaker."

Walter gave an understanding nod. Although he didn't believe a word, he chose not to comment.

"What have you got there?" asked Ray, keen to shift the focus away from his face. "Is it a kid's toy?"

"Hardly. These date back to the 1600s. John Turlington made them. He was a leading spectacle maker in London. You're familiar with Samuel Pepys?"

"The diarist? Yes. That is, I know a bit about him."

"Pepys bought these glasses from Turlington in 1666, believing the green tint would be gentler on his sore eyes."

Ray leaned in, taking a closer look. "What are the frames made from?"

"Leather." Walter noticed the frown on Ray's face and added, "A bit impractical, you might think, but it makes the spectacles lightweight and flexible."

"How do they stay on your face without the ear loops?"

"They don't."

Walter offered no further explanation. Ray shook his head in wonder. A pair of flimsy glasses with green lenses that sat precariously on the nose seemed a daft investment. Turlington must have been laughing all the way to the bank when Pepys left his shop.

The delicate way Walter held them made it clear that he prized them highly. Here was another rare, historical artifact for him to put in one of his many display cases and show off to colleagues, and this one was truly a piece of garbage.

"Are these glasses the reason you asked me over today?" asked Ray, slightly confused.

"No, these are just something I bought at an auction yesterday."

It was none of his concern how much money Walter had wasted on them. All the same, it didn't stop him wondering.

"I have more work for you—South Boston this time. You may be there for a week or a month, perhaps longer."

Ray nodded unenthusiastically.

"It's a delicate job; it requires the right temperament. I need someone like you who is well acquainted with the opposite sex. Someone charming and appealing and, well…persuasive." He watched with tight-lipped amusement as his employee's eyebrows ascended. "You seem to have a way with women. From what I hear, most of the broads in South Side have fallen for you at some point, and many have been particularly loath to part with you. They say that the Chicago River is mostly made up of the tears of broken-hearted young beauties who still pine for you."

Ray managed not to laugh. The last cherub-faced beauty he had charmed into his bed had almost bashed his brains out. "I'm not the Casanova you make me out to be, Walter. Far from it, actually. You'll find I'm no Rock Hudson. What's the job you have in mind? It sounds like you need me to seduce a girl."

"If that's what needs doing, then yes."

Ray rubbed his chin contemplatively. His eyes urged Walter to go on.

"I want you to tail a woman named Merriam Woodcroft. She's a secretary working at the Holy Trinity Church. On the surface, she's a sweet, angelic-faced young woman who seems right at home in a place of worship. Very prim and proper and very pretty. Actually, she's about as virtuous as the noxious reverend she's knocking about with. It's common knowledge that the pair regularly shack up together in a seedy motor court about ten miles north of Boston."

The job sounded more interesting, even if it meant a lengthy stay in Boston. "What's his story?"

"His name is Arnold Sinclair. He has a wife and child at home. For some reason, this doesn't much bother Merriam. Neither does she care that he is also a habitual thief and philanderer."

"How do you know this?"

"I sent a surveillance team to Boston last month to dig up what they could about him and pay close attention to his activities. They watched dozens of trucks and pickups pull up at the back lot of his church and collect and unload vast quantities of crates. There was no doubt about what sort of enterprise he was running. Likely, the reverend isn't just fencing stolen goods. Who knows what else he's mixed up in and the types of contraband he's smuggling into Boston."

"Why the sudden interest in Sinclair? Crooks in Boston are ten a penny."

"I received an anonymous tip-off telling me he had become a man of interest. They suggested I investigate him sooner rather than later. Rumor has it that others may soon take an interest in the reverend, so time is of the essence."

"What has he got that makes him so damn interesting, other than a pretty mistress and a vestry full of smuggled goods?"

"It appears he's made friends in the right places, and they're providing him with long-lost treasures—the sort that would fit perfectly in my private collection. Most interestingly, his suppliers have acquired a treasured piece of merchandise once estimated to be the most precious artifact ever discovered in a shipwreck: Hessman's Necklace. It is an emerald-studded 22-karat gold necklace discovered in the late Twenties by Jamaican marine explorer Herman Hessman. It's believed to have come from a Spanish galleon named San Salvatores that wrecked in 1590. Hessman swiftly sold his find to the Government of Jamaica. It was placed in the national museum, remaining there for some twenty years before it mysteriously went missing. A replica had been left in its place, so the theft wasn't discovered immediately. It's been ten years, with no culprits found and the necklace never retrieved."

"Interesting tale," said Ray, genuinely intrigued. "Am I correct in thinking that your surveillance team has found out where Sinclair is keeping it?"

The hint of a smile played on Walter's lips. Historical relics were his specialty. He had an expansive network of antiques hunters and art historians working with him, so over the years, some of the most incredible trinkets thought lost to the world had come into his possession. "That's the interesting part."

"How so?"

"The surveillance operation lasted three weeks, and yes, it proved successful. We need to get our hands on it to know if the necklace is genuine. However, they captured a tantalizing photograph with a telephoto lens. There's every indication that this may well be the real thing."

"May I see the photograph?"

Walter opened the top drawer of his desk and pulled out a large black-and-white picture. He slid it across the counter to Ray.

"Goodness!" Ray murmured, staring hard at the woman in the photograph. His eyes were focused squarely on the abundance of cleavage on display, so much so that he didn't even notice the jewelry around her neck.

"As you can see, she's wearing the treasure in their squalid love hideaway," Walter grumbled contemptuously. "My guess is that Sinclair keeps it in his safe at his church and brings it to her when they stay at this place. It's a big assumption, but that's what my gut instinct tells me. I wonder if she has any idea of its true value."

"I find it all a bit strange," agreed Ray. "It's surely clear to anyone that it's an extremely expensive antique. Hardly the sort of thing one brings to a place like that."

"Such reckless behavior makes me keen to take the ornament off her hands—or, rather, her neck," said Walter. "And as quickly as possible. I want you to get the necklace, Ray. By any means necessary."

"When do I leave?"

"Immediately."

———— ✦ ————

Although the fastest, most prudent way of getting to Boston was by plane, Ray's fear of flying prevented him from accepting the plane ticket Walter was desperate to book. The old man's angry protests did nothing to change his mind, and later that morning, Ray made a brief trip to the Bjorg Corporation headquarters, a leading rental company with an enormous lot on the city's outskirts. Walter was on good terms with the owner and told Ray to pick out the vehicle of his choice among John Bjorg's fleet of hundreds of passenger cars.

"Leave the Corvette in the garage and get yourself something less conspicuous," he had advised. "You'll want a speedy, reliable car. You may need to get out of Boston quickly once the job is over."

Ray had immediately responded with a broad, jubilant smile—the same one a racing car driver on the podium typically sports, especially when he's attempting to loop the fizzy liquid from his champagne bottle over the heads of photojournalists and into the mouth of his pin-up girlfriend. "A fast car, huh?" Ray had said with a little shake of the head, not quite believing he had heard Walter correctly. "I like it!"

"Not a fast car," the old man had corrected. "Something new and powerful, with a bit of horsepower, but nothing that belongs on a speedway, you hear!"

"No, of course not," Ray had agreed, although his mind was focused squarely on speed over dependability. In fact, his thoughts were already preoccupied with testing the accelerator and the steering and assessing how the mechanical beast took the bends.

Seeing the excited glint in Ray's eyes, Walter had added crossly: "Don't go for a blasted luxury sports car! I don't want to hear that you blazed off across America in a Ferrari. I know the way you drive, Ray. You'll have half the police force on your tail before you're out of Illinois, and then you'll flip the darn thing into a ditch. John Bjorg will never let me hear the end of it."

Ray had struggled to conceal his disappointment, as he was accustomed to speeding around town in a souped-up convertible. Walter's antagonistic glare had implied he ought to be shopping for a King Midget Model III rather than a Mercedes-Benz 300SL.

While Chuck, a slick-haired charmer with a carefully cultivated breezy manner, led him around the lot, Ray found himself tracking back to a Buick Roadmaster Riviera. He whistled with enthusiasm. "Now, this is an interesting brute."

"Ah, yes, the Roadmaster. I see you're a man with exquisite taste. Simplicity but flair, this car. Fixed roof, no B-pillars, and styled to look like a convertible with the top up." Chuck stopped to savor the desire in Ray's eyes. "Isn't she a beauty? Now, I won't lie to you," he said as an aside, "I've had my eye on this little number for quite some time. Such a delectable chariot. Just the car I would own if ever I were flush with cash. The newest Buick and their flagship vehicle."

He looked at the vehicle lovingly and then turned his gaze back to Ray. He was a ham actor who liked practicing his spiel in front of the mirror daily. He always came away liking what he saw. To him, the customer was much like an impressionable child.

"Smile big, swoon over a hulking great piece of gaudy garbage, and don't stop talking until you've persuaded the sucker to make a purchase," Chuck might say—if he was the frank and honest type. "Remember, they want to spend their pocket money on a toy. That's why they're here in the first place. Encourage them to spend all of it."

If he genuinely spoke his mind, he wouldn't be much of a salesman, though, and what a lovely, grasping, materialistic mind he was blessed with—consequently, he could afford any car in the lot he liked. "Hell, pick their damn pockets if you have to," was his private slogan. As for the vehicles in the lot, he didn't much like looking at them. The station wagon he owned was purely a practicality. His wife had insisted on it, and he didn't care to be seen with it. He much preferred motorbikes.

Ray didn't need more convincing to sign on the dotted line. He knew he wanted the Buick, and as his boss was footing the bill, the price meant nothing to him.

"Select a dependable vehicle manufactured by one of *The Big Three*," Walter had advised him. "General Motors, Ford, or Chrysler. Each of those is ideal. Stick to the popular models. You want something conventional."

Ray had fully intended to do as he was told, but when he saw the Roadmaster, all thoughts of being conservative went out of his head. He walked around the gleaming vehicle, admiring its body's dimensions and shape. It was an excellent, extravagantly sculpted piece of machinery—a top-of-the-range, two-door hardtop with the biggest body and engine. The side moldings made it seem longer than it was and gave the impression of squatting low to the ground. He especially liked the front fenders and reverse-slant side windows, not to mention the fine-tooth, whale-like front grill. He knew Walter would have disapproved of the chic car, which exuded luxury and sophistication. It was too new and almost too fancy to blend in with most other vehicles, but what did it matter? Walter had dreamed up a fake identity for him. He would be playing the part of a successful salesman traveling across the country. "Selling what, exactly?" he had asked Walter. Alas, the old man had shrugged off the question, avoiding offering suggestions. He had then provided Ray with a thick wad of papers containing sales slips, paid invoices, receipts, deposit slips, and canceled checks. There was also an accounting ledger among the documents.

"What's all this?" Ray had said with rising panic. "Homework?"

Walter referred to it as a prop, believing it might be helpful should Ray need to appear like a diligent salesman.

The explanation hadn't settled Ray's complaints. "But what does a salesman need all this junk for? What's he selling?"

"Just carry the damn thing about with you!" Walter had growled. "I'm sure at some point you'll be standing awkwardly, wishing you had something in your hands to fiddle with and make it seem like you have work. In those moments, this is exactly what you'll need. You can shuffle the pages about and look professional."

Ray hadn't argued further, even though he believed it was a silly idea.

"Should we move on and look at other more commonplace models?" Chuck asked slyly.

Ray shook his head. "Let's not. I've seen enough."

"My thoughts entirely. How do you feel about the Roadmaster Riviera?"

"It's as close as you can come to a Cadillac without buying one."

"And who doesn't like a Cadillac, right? Lovely color, too. Seminole red."

"Hand over the keys. I'll take her off your hands."

Chuck grabbed Ray's hand and shook it with such vigor that Ray was concerned the man might dislocate his shoulder. "She's all yours. Treat her with respect, and try not to knock her up."

———— ✦ ————

It was a tedious day spent confined to a car, traveling through one of the most uninspired routes in the Midwest. As he powered his handsome new vehicle across the dull landscape, he wondered what life must be like for those suckers stranded in one of these culture-starved towns. *It must be a gloomy existence*, he thought. *A life of disenchantment, of forlorn dreams, evenings devoted to the bottle, or to the weed, or to the hypodermic needle.*

He gave an involuntary shudder and was unaware that his foot was jammed down on the accelerator, imploring the vehicle to go faster, hoping to escape the endless highway and reach something that resembled civilization. The hours slowly slipped by, mile upon mile accumulating on his odometer, and then he was suddenly conscious of a flash of light in his interior mirror.

The speed at which he was going made it seem incredible to think someone was going even faster. He eased his foot off the accelerator, slowing the Buick, intending to let the car pass. *The speed demon behind him must be out of his mind*, he thought, convinced they must be drunk, or high, or just plain crazy.

A few moments later, the car behind loomed large in the mirror. Ray's eyes widened as he assessed the make and model, and then he gave a startled glance over his shoulder. The Ohio State Highway Patrol car markings were instantly recognizable. Ray let out a pained growl. With resignation, he applied the brake, steering his vehicle off the road. He hadn't heeded Walter's warning about speeding across America. *When Walter hears about this, he'll blow a gasket*, thought Ray.

He thumped the steering wheel in frustration. Evidently, he had given other motorists the impression he was attempting to set a new cross-country speed record. It was a force of habit, a mindless routine that could only land him in trouble.

And here was trouble.

Four

The '57 Chevy 150 two-door sedan pulled up behind him. While the driver took his sweet time getting out of the vehicle, Ray cursed his rotten luck, feeling sure that if he'd applied sufficient pressure on the accelerator, aiming for a steady 100 mph, he might have blazed through the entire state without anyone noticing. The idea of enforcing a speed restriction on an empty highway was infuriating. It was another sleazy scheme to line the pockets of lazy officials, a way to keep policemen employed at the expense of speedy motorists penalized for reaping the benefits of their gloriously fast cars.

The state trooper knocked on the driver's window, signaling Ray to roll down the glass. Ray's lack of haste made the officer slam his big knuckles on the windowpane as if testing his own strength.

Ray rotated the window crank with deliberate slowness. "There a problem?" he asked, projecting an air of innocence.

The plump officer studied him carefully and muttered, "Nice car. Looks new. Seeing how fast it goes?"

"No need. I know how fast it goes."

"Uh-huh. What's the top speed?"

"One hundred."

"Is that so?" the trooper said with a dry smile. It's a good thing you didn't test that out today. I might not have caught up with you."

"I don't know about that," Ray reflected. "You came up on me quickly back there. I figure you must have hit about that speed."

The trooper's cast-iron smirk immediately became unfixed, rapidly disappearing from his face altogether. "I see I found myself a wiseguy. Listen to this, smartmouth. I'm writing you a ticket."

"What for?"

"What for?" repeated the trooper with a laugh, although his eyes were completely devoid of humor, and his mouth gave the impression that he was snarling rather than laughing. "If your foot had stayed on the gas any longer, you would have topped out at one ten."

"Says who?"

"Says me, that's who."

The trooper stared at Ray with startled annoyance. "Say, you been drinking?"

"No," responded Ray impatiently. "I could use a whisky right now, though."

"You make sure you stay off the booze. A fast car like this and a reckless driver at the wheel with hooch in him is a recipe for trouble."

"Sure," nodded Ray compliantly. "Can I go now?"

"No, you can't go. You wait here while I fill out the ticket."

Ray watched with resentment as the cop wrote up a ticket with the hood of his gleaming new sedan doubling as the trooper's writing desk.

"Sonofabitch," Ray said under his breath.

When the cop finally allowed him to go on his way, Ray struggled to contain his anger. He sped away a little faster than he ought to have, and soon, his speed climbed back toward 100 mph. He wanted to escape the state quickly and put that unpleasant incident behind him.

After a full day of driving, he reached Youngstown, Ohio, as the sun began to set. He was almost halfway through his journey and nearing the point where he contemplated facing his fear of flying.

As he made his way into the downtown district, he surveyed the dark, forbidding shadows that clung to the tall buildings on Central Square. The heart of Youngstown looked just as Walter had described it: a lovely place affectionately termed "Murdertown, U.S.A." Walter insisted on calling it by its other nickname: "Mob Stranglehold." It was a place of gangland slayings; this was one of America's most dangerous areas and a haven for organized crime. A city where all manner of tough-guy crime thrived, from extensive bribery and bombings to bullets to the back of the head. In other words, Walter might define it, in glowing terms, as "a swell place to stay."

———— ✦ ————

Ray stopped at the Slate Gray Motor Hotel, an eyesore just around the corner of the main drag. His no-frills room was stark and depressing, with stained curtains and a cracked mirror in the bathroom. The bed was about the size of a lounger and offered much the same level of comfort. Ray suspected that any attempt to flip the mattress over would result in it falling to pieces, leaving behind handfuls of bedbugs and cigarette ash.

For all its faults, he didn't mind his digs. The price was low, and the location was ideal. On top of that, he found the old man serving on the front desk to be a hoot. When Ray asked for a room, the toothless old-timer quoted him an hourly rate, giving Ray a full understanding of the hotel's clientele.

When it turned eight o'clock, Ray took a folded slip of paper out of his pocket and returned to the lobby to use the telephone. Walter had given him the name of a reliable contact in Youngstown who viewed himself as something akin to a concierge. Walter had depicted him as the best supplier in the Midwest, able to provide whatever information or equipment Ray needed.

Ray dropped a coin in the box and worked the dial on the telephone.

"This Len?" he asked when he heard a male voice on the line.

"Who's asking?"

"Ray Stokes. Walter Cartwell gave me your number."

"I doubt that," came the unexpected response. "Lose my number, pal."

"Wait," urged Ray. "I need your help. I need supplies."

"Then go to a hardware store," Len snapped before hanging up.

Ray tapped the receiver against his chin, pondering his next course of action. Realizing he didn't have one, he dropped another coin in the box and redialed Len's number.

"Didn't you hear me earlier, pal?" snapped Len when he heard Ray's voice.

"Walter said to call you if I needed anything. He'll hate it when I tell him you didn't live up to your reputation."

"Yeah? What reputation?"

"He said you were the best merchant in the whole Midwest. Dependable was the word he used." Ray allowed a wily pause and then added snidely, "Guess he didn't know the word's meaning. Probably meant disreputable. I'll move on to the next name on my list. Walter won't enjoy hearing he was wrong, but I'm sure he's heard it often enough."

"Ray Stokes. That what you said your name was?"

"That's right."

"You're one of Walter's antique hunters, right?"

"You could put it that way."

"How's Walter these days?"

An honest opinion would include the words *guarded*, *self-centered*, and *dour*. However, lately, the old coot had fallen out of his cloud of serenity and become an animated, prattling bag of excitement, clamoring for an eye-popping hunk of old treasure that Ray had a strong feeling might well turn out to be a cheap stocking filler. Not wanting to admit as much to Len, he simply said, "He's as acquisitive and determined as ever. Utterly focused on perfecting his collections."

"Still after that lost Rubens?" asked Len with only casual interest. "The name of the piece escapes me."

"Diana and two nymphs bathing surprised by a Satyr."

"Yeah, that's it."

"He's still after it, but who isn't?"

Len responded with a dissatisfied grunt. "What about the Raphael?"

Interesting question, thought Ray, loath to discuss that particular piece. "What about it?"

"I hear it's been recovered."

"You heard wrong."

"You're saying it's not hanging in that dingy secret chamber behind the bookcase in Walter's library?"

Ray scratched his chin contemplatively. Walter had shown him the secret chamber on a few rare occasions to show off magnificent, highly sought-after artifacts he had miraculously acquired. The valuable pieces disappeared as quickly as they arrived, changing hands swiftly like old, crumpled dollar bills. Ray felt privileged to have seen High Renaissance art up close. He had once seen a sumptuous painting by Alessandro Bonvicino—better known as Moretto da Brescia (the Moor of Brescia)—that only a handful of people knew existed. Sadly, Ray had never seen the lost painting by Raffaello Sanzio da Urbino.

"It wasn't hanging there the last time I looked," he carelessly muttered. "You and Walter must be especially close if you know about his hidden chamber."

"Oh, yeah, sure. We're as close as brothers," Len said proudly, bringing a smirk to Ray's lips.

Ray had heard Walter talk of an older brother named Herbert, and it was not with any iota of fondness. Apparently, the two once-close brothers had fallen out some years earlier because of a bottle of Château Mouton Rothschild. Or, rather, quite a few bottles of the celebrated Bordeaux wine.

While staying at Walter's home during the month of June, looking after the luxurious property while his brother was on holiday in the Adirondacks, Herbert had indulged heavily in food and fine wine. He had gluttonously raided Walter's pantry, eating only the best things he could lay his hands on, and most unforgivably, he had gone through Walter's wine cellar with astounding intemperance. A wedding party full of lushes couldn't have devoured more alcohol than Herbert. He showed no restraint during his month's stay, and by the sounds of it, he must have been inebriated the entire time.

Walter had a particularly fine wine cellar and was hoarding some of the best French wines in America. As he had made it clear to his brother before he went on vacation, there were bottles for everyday consumption and bottles for special occasions. Then there were bottles that were so valuable, so sought after, that no wine collector was ever tempted to uncork them.

Perhaps Walter should have explained that part a little better. As Walter was exploring the Adirondack Region—taking healthy hikes in the mountains, as per the instructions of his personal doctor, who was concerned that unless Walter dramatically changed his unhealthy lifestyle, his generous patient might not live long enough to provide the doctor with sufficient income to put his youngest son through college—Herbert was drinking for the pair of them, and rapidly increasing his chances of an early death. He had started with the everyday wines but quickly tired of those and moved on to the special occasion wines. After those, he had worked his way through the rare, vintage wines, guzzling imported wonders of the world that had a market value of thousands of dollars. Carelessly, heartlessly, he had gobbled prized pieces, dismantling what great wine connoisseurs had previously described as an enviable collection and reducing it to something humbler.

When Walter returned home, he was incensed by the damage Herbert had done. The shock and anger brought on by the sight of all those empty wine bottles meant that any improvements to his health were short-lived. In fact, when he saw the empty Château Mouton Rothschild 1945, a bottle with a "V" for victory on the label, celebrating the Allied victory, Walter experienced an excruciating migraine and savage pains in his stomach.

In one month, Herbert had rid his brother's cellar of one-fifth of its stock and brought the value of Walter's wine collection back to where it had been some ten years earlier. To make matters worse, Walter soon discovered a discarded bottle of Bouchard Père et Fils Musigny from 1945 lying on its side near the fireplace in his study. Not all of the bottle's contents had made it down his brother's throat. Some exceedingly good red wine had spilled onto Walter's antique Persian vase rug, causing the old man to weep like a jilted schoolgirl.

The desire to punish Herbert was intense, and it took a Herculean effort to refrain from beating his brother to death with the stoking iron he had instinctively seized from the poker stand by the fireplace. A generous supply of barbiturates took the edge off his lust to behead his brother, and he made a deal with his psychiatrist to banish Herbert from his life and never speak to him again.

He also vowed never to revisit the Adirondacks.

Ray kept the story to himself. It wasn't his nature to talk about Walter's private life, and it wouldn't be prudent either.

"As you and Walter are so close, you won't mind helping him with his latest treasure hunt," he told Len. "I have a small shopping list of things I'd like."

"You're in Youngstown?"

"Yes."

"For how long?"

"One night. I'll continue east tomorrow."

"Okay, shoot."

After parroting the things on his list, he said, "I'll take whatever you can lay your hands on. Functional is fine, as long as it's not junk."

"I only deal in quality merchandise."

"Can you supply me with everything tonight?"

"Let me place a few calls and see what I can do. Sit tight. I'll contact you later."

"How long will that take? I haven't eaten a thing since noon," grumbled Ray. "All I can think about right now is getting out of this pen and going in search of something coated in batter and dripping with grease. Put enough hot sauce on it, and I'll eat just about anything. About how long do you reckon I'll need to sit tight?"

Len said diplomatically, "I'll make some calls shortly. I'm not a magician, despite what you may have heard. I don't expect to have anything for you for at least the next few hours. Say, as it's a nice evening, you should hold off eating fried food and take a walk. You're in a good city, so make the most of your time here. Where are you staying?"

"The Slate Gray Motor Hotel."

"Nice choice. The beds are comfy, and the rooms are so clean that a cockroach wouldn't dare set foot in the joint."

Ray turned his nose up, suspecting Len had never stayed in anything better than a doss house. The cockroach comment played on his mind, though, and his eyes automatically wandered around the lobby. He imagined he saw cockroaches scuttling across the walls and escaping beneath the door.

Len cleared his throat and continued to speak. His light, tuneful voice came as a welcome distraction. "If it's a quick bite you want, head over to Madam Rousseau's on Commerce Street. It's a coffee and sandwich restaurant attached to the Palace."

Ray stopped scrutinizing the walls. "There's a palace in Youngstown."

"It's a movie house."

"Oh. Yes, I think I passed some movie houses on the drive here."

"You would have gone down Federal Street. There are three movie houses around there, and a fourth, a nice-looking building called the Palace, is a block away on Commerce. Dates back to nineteen twenty-six. It had a different name back then and wasn't set up for movies the way it is now. Check out its lobby and the balconies on the upper levels if you have time. Lots of big singers and vaudeville acts performed there in its heyday. The Andrews Sisters, Laurel and Hardy, Bill 'Bojangles' Robinson. The war years brought Frank Sinatra, Lena Horne, and other top singers here. My sis met Frank once."

"Oh yeah?"

"Says he pinched her on the tush."

Ray thanked him and read out the telephone number to his room. "I'll be back in an hour," he said.

"Take your time. Madam Rousseau's serves great desserts, and the waitress, Madeline, is a real doll. She knows how to satisfy the most ravenous of men."

Ray's stomach cried out with hunger as he hung up the phone.

Ten minutes later, he pulled on his jacket and exited his room, walking briskly, eager to get to his car and locate the restaurant. Although he liked variety in his diet, he was no gastronome, and tonight, he was in the mood for classic American cuisine, not overly caring how it was served. He was willing to eat his shoelaces if they were smothered in enough ketchup.

When he stepped out of the hotel, the sunlight dazzled him. It was gloriously warm, and he contemplated taking off his jacket. His chalk-stripe sports coat went remarkably well with his button-down vest and dark brown slacks, making him loath to remove it. He was a man who invariably chose fashion over functionality, the type to layer up in stylish clothes in hot weather and who was reluctant to hide his chic outfit under a heavy coat in winter. He didn't mind that he was conspicuously dressed and that his fashionable clothes, which were wasted on Youngstown, singled him out as a tourist.

In contrast to his eye-catching attire and the cheery weather, the atmosphere around the Slate Gray Motor Hotel was decidedly chilly. The dingy-looking parking lot out front was enough to give anyone the creeps. Worse, a posse of youths hanging around the small cluster of cars made it look even grimmer. They were gathered around Ray's Buick, puffing on cigarettes and trying to look tough. One was slouched up against the chrome bumper, gesturing to the others with his hands. The way his body was hugging the car gave the impression he owned it.

The buoyancy went out of Ray during his walk to the car, his pleasant smile rapidly morphing into a pout. He pulled his car keys from his pocket, making an extravagant show of them. The etched apprehension on his face became more pronounced as he slid the key into the lock. The insolent brute resting his elbow on the hood ornament glanced fleetingly at Ray, and the only expression on his face was idle curiosity. His friends stared vacantly at the newcomer, oblivious to Ray's glowering face and averse to moving out of his way. Ray's presence was merely a mild distraction, and in an instant, they resumed their conversation, ignoring him completely.

Ray held his tongue and climbed into the vehicle, aggressively closing the door. He attempted to go about his routine as if everything was normal, pretending they were a figment of his imagination and would vanish the moment he stopped fretting. He put the key in the ignition and started the car, and in his mind, the teenagers drifted away like dark, portentous clouds. When he stepped on the gas, he felt better. Everything felt right. Everything felt back to normal.

There was an intense outburst of confusion as the vehicle jolted forward. The youngsters scampered out of the way, but the buffoon against the hood was too slow to react. The vehicle shunted him in the back, and he stumbled forward, tripping over and disappearing beneath the car.

Five

Ray gasped and slammed his foot on the brake. His body lurched forward, hugging the steering column, the taste of bile strong in his mouth. He was convinced he had stopped the car a split second too late, and his mind conjured up an image of the victim's mangled face—jaw snapped, an eye dislocated from its socket, blood leaking from a severe gash across the scalp.

Mercifully, the braking system on Buicks had been enhanced quite recently, with a suspended brake pedal added in the past year. Power brakes, though an optional feature, were installed in this 1957 Roadmaster model. He was aware of this detail thanks to Chuck, the talkative salesman at the Bjorg Corporation headquarters, although it didn't greatly ease his mind in this moment of crisis.

As Ray clutched the steering wheel tightly, unable to release his grip, extraneous minutiae about the width of the brake shoes and the iron drums distracted him. *How rapidly do the brake shoes fade as a result of emergency braking?* It was infuriating nonsense that wouldn't even interest a mechanic, but the asinine thought helped calm his nerves. While he stared wildly out of the windshield, observing every little detail across the street, sudden movement beside the left front wheel revealed the young man had somehow escaped damage in the nick of time and now stood by the side of the car, visibly shaken but seemingly unharmed. The wild fright in Ray's eyes was reflected in the young man's quaking face.

Ray recovered quickly, returning his foot to the gas pedal, keen to make a speedy departure. He accelerated rapidly out of the parking lot without sparing a glance in his side mirrors or noticing the two youths who chased after the car, determined to inflict damage but unable to catch up with him. It was a decidedly nifty getaway and, for once, a decent bit of driving. Although his heart was still racing, he managed to steady his thoughts and turn a deaf ear to the rising indignation ten meters behind him, where shock and horror had given way to anger and revenge.

Once on the main road, he began to put a positive spin on the unpleasant incident. The near tragedy would become an amusing anecdote, he determined, as well as a social commentary on the hazards for inner-city motorists posed by delinquent youths with substance abuse disorders.

His foot eased off the gas pedal, and he steered the car sedately toward the city's commercial center. The white columns of the Stambaugh Auditorium and the eighteen-story Metropolitan Tower caught his eye. Peeping at him from all directions as he trundled around West Federal Street was the distinctive white clock tower on the Home Savings and Loan Building.

He was especially vigilant during the journey to Rousseau's, wary of pedestrians and on the lookout for cops. Having acquired a traffic violation early in his trip, he had concerns about further infringements on his driver's license. Walter had assigned him the role of traveling salesman, making an out-of-state plate acceptable, but Ray had second thoughts about sticking to the plan. Was his Illinois license plate a hindrance, a beacon for undesirables, a magnet for law enforcement? The local youth regarded the hood of his car as a comfy alternative to the park bench. Highway police saw it as an office desk. Riffraff was drawn to his vehicle like fireflies to a porch light, and it was only a matter of time before graffiti artists used it as a canvas for their next project.

He decided to switch it with a Massachusetts plate when he reached Boston. Until then, he would have to attune his mind to becoming an exemplary driver. One who obeyed speed limits and didn't plow into pedestrians.

He parked near the Palace Theater, noticing the neighborhood was especially quiet. Hunger pangs made him hurry into the restaurant next door to the movie theater. It was roomy and had a timeworn feel that seemed deliberate, as if management wanted to cling to fond memories of the boomtown days when Youngstown was a thriving, prosperous place and Rousseau's was hip and relevant. Ray gazed around at the dozen customers scattered around the room, though none of them paid him any attention.

There was no hostess, and the waitress was engrossed in deep conversation with the cashier, so he seated himself in a booth and studied the table menu as if preparing for an exam. Fortunately, the waitress was far more attentive, fussing around him as if he were a dignitary. Len's glowing praise of the wait staff proved fair. Madeline was as sweet as the syrup on his pancakes, and Ray's only complaint was that her constant chatter kept him from his food.

When he exited Rousseau's, he felt like he had eaten a week's worth of meals. It didn't stop him from hitting some trendy bars afterward, though. Nothing kept him from soaking up city nightlife.

The fact that he cut the festivities short and returned to his hotel before dawn was nothing short of miraculous. The fact that he was not alone held no surprise.

———— ✦ ————

The emphatic knock at the door curtailed Ray's thoughts of showering. His first thought was that the maid was arriving to turn down the bed. Although, gauging the Slate Gray Motor Hotel's standards, the image that formed in his head was a mature woman in a lewd maid's outfit soliciting her services.

When Ray threw back the sheets and rolled out of bed, he hadn't the faintest idea where he had thrown his underwear and didn't care to conduct a search. Instead, he grabbed a clean bath towel from the back of the chair and wrapped it around his waist. The knock at the door grew more forceful, with less knuckle and more fist, making him wonder if it was actually a house dick investigating a crime. He opened the door, prepared for trouble.

A stocky man with thinning gray hair and a smile as crooked as his nose was leaning against the doorframe. "Ray Stokes?"

"Uh-huh. Who's asking?"

"Len Cleary. We spoke on the phone. Sorry to get here so late."

Ray nodded contentedly and beckoned him into the room, noticing with disapproval the older man's threadbare jacket. Len's shoes were old and scuffed, too, and his baggy pants seemed several sizes too large for him. It made Ray wonder if everything the man possessed had been acquired secondhand. The look of his tatty shirt certainly gave the impression it was procured from a flea market.

As Len moved past Ray, he looked dubiously around the cramped quarters. It had the usual furnishing: bed, wardrobe, dresser. Other than a hard chair, there wasn't much to trip over. Deciding against the chair, he plonked himself down on the bed, resting his tan briefcase on his lap.

"You got a chance to eat, I hope?"

Ray closed the door and perched on the edge of the dresser. "I followed your recommendation and went to Rousseau's."

"How was it?"

"Very satisfying."

"Thought you'd like it," said Len, looking pleased with himself. "Serves large, tasty helpings, doesn't it?"

"It was much as I expected," Ray said less enthusiastically. "The service was as you described it."

"Warm, efficient?"

"Attractive and buxom," corrected Ray. "And very accommodating."

Len was suddenly aware of faint noises emanating from the bathroom. He shot a troubled glance at the bathroom door, listening to the strong hiss of water as the shower snapped on. His wary gaze shifted to Ray. "You got company?"

"Just some girl I picked up."

"A call girl?"

"A waitress. Actually, the one at Rousseau's you kindly recommended."

"Madeline?" responded Len, oddly bothered.

"That's right. I must thank you. She was better than expected."

Len looked flabbergasted. His watery blue eyes widened when he heard the sound of her voice in the bathroom. She had started to sing.

"Holy cow. Been here five minutes, and now you're courting Madeline."

"Courting her!" Ray was tickled by the man's quaint way of putting it.

Len studied him a little more intently. "You in search of antiques or on the hunt for a wife?"

Ray practically winced at the notion. "Can't say I'm ever on the hunt for a wife."

"Does Madeline know that?" snapped Len disapprovingly. "The idea of you leading a good girl along doesn't sit well with me."

Ray's eyes narrowed. "What are you, her father? The local preacher, perhaps?"

Len gave a contrite shrug and scratched his thick neck. "If you wanted a broad, you should have said. I could have called the brothel and had them send you someone."

"You the local pimp too?"

"I can supply a sleazebag with whatever he wants," Len responded hotly. "I'd rather play king pimp to tourists than have them sully the remaining respectable girls we have in the community."

Although angry at the caustic remark, Ray couldn't help but feel a strange reverence toward his pug-nosed visitor. "Let's look at the nice gifts you've brought this contemptible sleazebag?"

Len duly slid the latches on the briefcase outward to release the clasp, then lifted the lid and rummaged inside. He removed a switchblade and passed it to Ray. "This is an authentic Italian-made seven-inch stiletto knife. It has a beautiful dragon design handle with stainless steel bolsters and a satin finished kris blade."

Ray scrutinized it, turning it over and admiring the ornate white dragons carved into the hilt. He adjusted his grip and pressed the button in the handle, causing a gleaming, wavy blade to spring out.

"Very nice," he muttered, running his finger gently along the blade, appreciating its sharpness. It felt good in his hand. Light, yet deadly, and much more expedient in confined spaces than other weapons.

Len foraged around in the briefcase and produced a sturdy leather zip case. "Here, a traditional set of pin tumbler lockpicks," he said, offering it to Ray.

Ray put the switchblade down on the dresser and received the small leather pouch from him. He unzipped it and carefully examined the line of picks.

"This set includes seven picks and six tension wrenches of varying widths," said Len. "You'd know better than me. I haven't a clue how those things work."

Ray removed the Hook Pick, the most common lock pick for single pin picking, and brought it up to his eyes for close inspection. Satisfied, he returned it to the case. The thin picks on either side of it were variations of the same classic pick.

"Well, what do you think? Those things good enough for you?" asked Len.

"They'll do."

"As for that postiche you wanted…"

Ray's eyebrows ascended sharply at the sound of the unfamiliar word. "A pos what?"

"A postiche," said Len with a thin smirk. "You asked me for a hairpiece, didn't you?"

"Ah, the toupee. Yes. You have it? A good one, I hope."

"Listen, this isn't the type of merchandise one gets asked for every day of the week. I don't have some backstreet barber with a loom or what-have-you spinning hairpieces in their shop for me. This sort of product takes time to come by. All I could manage at short notice was this little black headpiece."

Ray carefully took the petite wig from him and examined it diligently. The hair, darker and softer than he had imagined, was medium length and bushy. He pictured a young Japanese woman with a long head of silky hair that extended to her ankles. Was this whose head it had once belonged to, he wondered?

"I've absolutely no idea where the hair comes from," said Len, as if reading Ray's mind. "It's made by hand, although I doubt it was made in this country. Imported from overseas, most likely. It could be European, could be Asian. I'm told that England and France were the major hubs for this kind of thing, but that's going back some. Nineteenth and twentieth century, I should think, when wigs were the rage. Can't say there is a demand for these things nowadays. This particular hairpiece is from a theater company. Your guess is as good as mine as to the actor's role."

"Actually, I would have thought it was worn by an actress."

"It's a man's wig," said Len defensively. "At least, that's what I'm told."

"You're sure about that? It doesn't look especially feminine, but it also doesn't look like it was designed for a man," Ray protested. "At any rate, it doesn't much matter either way. As long as it doesn't appear out of place on my head, it's of no consequence."

"Thinking of treading the boards?" asked Len with a sneer.

Ray tossed the hairpiece onto the bed without much

enthusiasm. "Hardly."

"I'm assuming this is another part of your intended costume?" said Len, passing him a pair of black spectacles.

Ray opened the temples and slipped the glasses onto his face. He looked up at Len, who was nodding with approval.

"They suit you."

"Do they?" said Ray with surprise. He removed the square, horn-rimmed spectacles. "Well, I may not need these or the wig. Just a precautionary measure."

Len was eying him inquisitively. "Thinking of attending an auction in disguise?"

"Precisely," said Ray. "Always good to maintain anonymity at those places."

The blatant lie didn't fool Len for a minute, but he knew better than to pry. For his own sake, the less he knew about his client's affairs, the better.

Ray put the glasses on the bedside table. He didn't need spectacles and hoped he wouldn't have to put them on his face again, not caring much for their look.

Len sniffed with indifference and rummaged around in his briefcase once more. "Now for the pièce de résistance," he said, suddenly more animated.

He pulled out a handgun, holding it charily.

"Ah, the Smith & Wesson," murmured Ray approvingly.

The way Len's eyes glistened persuaded Ray that he was a gun enthusiast. "A .357 Magnum, as requested. You need any pointers on using it?"

Len's abnormal grip on the gun made Ray believe he had never discharged one. He was probably too old to have held a Buck Rogers Rocket Pistol or the Disintegrator model, but perhaps he had used a BB gun at some point.

"That won't be necessary," said Ray, taking the revolver from him. He held it by the grip and checked to make sure it wasn't loaded.

"It comes with twenty cartridges and this cowhide leather shoulder holster." Len held up the holster for Ray to examine. The box of cartridges was in his other hand. "The holster hangs vertically under the left shoulder for maximum concealment and comfort."

Ray glanced at the holster but didn't bother to inspect it. "It looks fine. Pass me the cartridges, will you."

Len handed them to him, saying, "You just let me know if there's anything else I can get you."

As Ray opened the box and checked the labeling on the carton as well as the round, Len returned the holster to the case.

"Always happy to help out Walter and his associates. It's been a while since we talked. Glad I'm still top of his list of suppliers," he said, trying to gauge if there might be some return business.

Ray mumbled thanks, but his attention was now squarely focused on the gun.

"You know, Walter and I go back a long way," continued Len. "We were working together in the nineteen thirties. He ever tell you about our involvement with the Reynolds gang? Dark and dangerous days, those. We were a small link in a large chain of traders helping to steal crime-syndicate handbooks."

Ray ignored him. In fact, he was unaware the man had spoken.

Len sighed and started to rearrange the contents of the briefcase. Then he lifted the case off his lap and transferred it to the bed, leaving it open. He remarked, "You can also have this nice tan cowhide briefcase if you like."

Ray looked up, suddenly reminded of the man's presence. "Say, that's a nice case," he remarked, putting the pistol on the dresser next to the switchblade. He shifted off the dresser and went over to the bed. "I thought I saw…yes, here we are," he said delightedly, hoisting a Johnnie Walker Red Label bottle of blended Scotch whiskey from the briefcase. "Just what I need."

"You asked for a bottle of whiskey, so I got you the best. It will brighten your night. Or what's left of it, that is."

"That it will," agreed Ray, cradling the bottle like a first-time father handling a newborn.

"There's also a tin of aspirin in there, in case you quaff the whole darn bottle in one sitting and need something to help you face the day."

"If I do that, I'll need more than aspirin to fix me."

"Can't help you there. I advise you to leave a couple of shots in the bottle for the morning. Hair of the dog is always the best remedy for a hangover." As he went to the door, he said, "Safe travels, and all the best with your quest."

Ray held up a finger. "Just a minute."

He went to his suitcase and removed a fat, sealed envelope from the front pocket. "Here, take this," he said, throwing the weighty package to Len.

The over-stuffed envelope bounced out of Len's hands and landed heavily on the floor, bursting open on impact and spilling twenty-dollar bills across the carpet. The man's hand-eye coordination was something to marvel at—his catching ability might give Yogi Berra the willies. In point of fact, Len didn't like baseball, but he had contacts who made a good living from sports memorabilia, and chances were he could get hold of Berra's catcher's mitt from 1951 when the player won his first AL MVP award, and probably at a price so low that people would call it "a steal."

"Darn clumsy hands," groaned Len. "Never was competent at sports."

He fell to his knees and started gathering up the money. The mass of twenties made his eyes bulge.

"I'll leave you to it," said Ray, heading toward the bathroom. "Thanks for the supplies."

"Give my best to Walter," said Len. "Tell him that…"

The bathroom door clicked shut, and moments later, Len heard the shower curtain being drawn back, and Madeline let out a startled cry. Len was about to charge into the room, but

Madeline's hearty laugh stopped him. The laughter turned to joyful murmurs.

Len sighed and began returning the cash to the envelope. While Madeline hummed cheerily in the shower, he thought about the switchblade and the picks and the gun. He glanced briefly at the items on the dresser as he made his way out of the hotel room, curious about the task Walter had assigned Ray and speculating about the value of whatever relic Ray was hunting down.

Six

The Johnnie Walker Red Label on his dresser became an unfortunate temptation that made leaving Youngtown much harder. Six hours later, as Ray knelt by the side of his car, struggling to make it to his feet without retching, he wished he had never twisted the cap off the bottle. His alcohol tolerance was high, and his nightly consumption was impressive. Sickness and routine headaches hadn't plagued him until quite recently, though now, his uncurbed, decadent lifestyle had become a problem needing immediate containment.

Ray lay a hand on the fender, propping himself up. He was huddled against a hubcap, feeling like he was about to project the contents of his sour stomach across the parking lot. As sick as he was, he knew it was unwise to waylay his trip. His slowness in getting to Boston was dangerous, especially given Walter's unforgiving nature. The old man treated his employees well, often making those on his payroll believe a friendship existed, but he didn't easily forgive errant behavior, and typically, he exacted some sort of revenge on people who transgressed. There were stories of vicious assaults and vandalism of property; debts were imposed, and assets seized. Some individuals even went missing, with hints about their grim fate serving as frightening warnings to others. The fact that Walter had paid Ray a lot of money to find the necklace cautioned the young criminal against making foolish decisions that might undermine his mission. The high reward emphasized

Walter's desire for the artifact, and it also intimated that there would be a hefty price to pay if Walter didn't get it.

What form the punishment would take was not something Ray wanted to dwell on, and the fact he hadn't failed Walter before made him dead keen to maintain his perfect record. Whether the reverend's unique curio was authentic or merely a vintage gewgaw, it didn't much matter. When the wealthy collector wanted something, his flunkies knew to get him it posthaste. Ray's circuitous route would ultimately test the old man's patience, but his goal was to make up for lost time once he reached Boston and rely on his tried and tested expertise in little matters like burglary, trickery, and cruelty.

He made another effort to get to his feet, fighting further nausea. The grievous ache in his head was abysmal, but he knew it would be a mistake to give in to the hangover. He was battling the clock, experienced enough to know that Walter would check his progress daily, growing more frustrated with each passing day.

It was then that Ray noticed two deep scratches along the side of the vehicle, defacing his expensive Buick. They were malicious grooves inflicted with purpose. Some punk who had doubtless been dropped on his head repeatedly as a kid had scratched the car up good, making Ray swear furiously. Alas, all that did was make his head hurt more.

When Ray pulled open the driver's door and dropped into the seat, he felt like he might be unable to steer the car out of the parking lot without incident, and the last thing he wanted was another interaction with the police. He let out a deep sigh, plagued by the realization that he could hardly see straight. There were six hundred torturous miles to go until he reached the finishing line, and really, that was just the starting point for his mission. A mission without a fully formed plan of action. So far, the only concrete detail was his accommodation. Walter had booked him a room at the Hotel Buckminster, a historic, relatively inexpensive hotel in Kenmore Square. From there, he would monitor Merriam and

Sinclair over the ensuing days, forming a clearer understanding of their relationship. Ray figured that there had to be something other than sexual allure that compelled a beautiful woman to become the mistress of a crooked man of the cloth. Everything about their relationship confused him and made him skeptical. What made her choose the reverend and not a more desirable specimen of the human race? Judging by her superlative looks, Merriam could have her pick of the many handsome, unmarried men in Boston. Was she as appealing as her picture suggested, though? Or was there something dark and unpleasant about her personality that made her unappetizing to potential suitors? An all-too-apparent personality disorder, perhaps. Was she a crazed lunatic, a bitter and twisted psychopath? Was she drawn to Sinclair because of a perverse fascination with black-hearted villains? What hold did he have over her?

Ray was keen to find out the ugly truth. Mostly, though, he was eager to be done with the assignment. As pretty and lively as the city was, he didn't care for the citizens of Massachusetts. Previous visits made him believe that the place was overpopulated with rude and arrogant people with an unhealthy self-interest that bordered on narcissism.

He put the key in the ignition and started the car. A long day loomed, and his assignment wouldn't truly begin until the sun had set. While he stared out of the windshield, uncertain how he would concentrate on the road and avoid an accident, the purr of the engine offered comfort.

———— ✦ ————

It was dark and lightly raining when Ray finally reached his destination. After navigating his way through the main hub of the city, he located a convenient parking lot close to Fenway Park and scurried through the muddy puddles on the triangular intersection of Beacon Street and Brookline Avenue until he reached the hotel.

Walter had recommended Hotel Buckminster because of its historical importance. He didn't care that the hotel dated back to 1897; he merely derived pleasure from the fact that this was the place where the notorious Chicago Black Sox scandal of 1919 was hatched. Ray had little interest in baseball, so the high-profile match-fixing scandal, where eight members of the Chicago White Sox were accused of intentionally losing the World Series, interested him about as much as the prospect of watching a Red Sox game.

Once in his small, humble room, Ray tossed his coat on a peacock blue wing chair, kicked off his blue and white canvas saddle shoes, and threw himself down on the bed. A soft moan escaped from his parched lips, and within ten minutes, he was out cold, a sonorous snore reverberating around the room.

He didn't move again until mid-morning, and then dread lured him out of bed and back into his shoes. He prided himself on his level of success, and the thought of failure disturbed his composure.

After taking a light breakfast, he traveled to South Boston to scope out the drab residential neighborhood, spending most of his time frequenting the local old-school diners and taverns to establish himself as a new member of the community. There was a strong Irish-American presence, and one of the locals, a beady-eyed youth with a pronounced limp, took a shine to him. Ray stuck to the phony profile Walter had invented to explain his temporary move to Boston, and soon, the boy had come up with a nickname for Ray—the Chicago Trader. Ray was tickled by the tag, and by the time he left "Southie," as people liked to call it, he felt a step closer to being perceived as one of the regulars.

The following day, he returned to the area to snoop around the century-old Holy Trinity Church and its grounds. This was his opportunity to assess the various security flaws, hoping to gain entry to the church later that night. Given that it was a building used for public Christian worship, he didn't imagine a sophisticated security system would be in place.

When he arrived, he found tough-looking riffraff milling about outside the façade, looking like a litter of vagrants making use of the empty public benches. It was hard to tell if they had an affiliation with the church, and he made the mistake of neglecting to pay them adequate attention while he stood outside gazing up at the belfry.

He noticed an elderly lady mount the front steps and pull on the imposing front door. She made her way into the building untroubled, and so he concluded it was safe enough to make his move. He hadn't entered a church since boyhood. Once every year, his mother had compelled him to go with her to their local parish church on Christmas Eve for the late-night service. It was a holiday tradition. A Midnight Mass with carols and scripture readings, and he had always considered it the low point of the holidays. Later, as an adult, he had never felt the urge to want to sit on an uncomfortable pew again, not even at Christmastime. The thought of leafing through a bible and listening to a clergyman give a longwinded sermon always sapped his mental fortitude, and it did so again at this precise moment. While he approached the porch, he felt his feet becoming leaden and a yawn forming in his mouth. With every step, he questioned the wisdom of opening the door. It reached the point where he wasn't sure he had the strength to go through with it, not now, not ever. The sight of a hymn book might actually send him into depression. His sole intention was to zip around the nave, taking in as much as he could before he lost the will to live. A quick in and out, and hopefully that would be enough to gauge the operation. Yet no matter how short his visit, he dreaded setting foot inside, tasting the musty air and enduring the gloomy confines. He rather hoped a service wouldn't be in progress.

As it turned out, he didn't get the chance to see beyond the carved entrance. Two swarthy individuals descended on him, briskly obstructing his path when he was within three feet of the door.

"Hey, buddy, can you spare some change?" said one of them, coercing him to a halt.

The man was dressed in shabby, ill-fitting clothes, his grimy fingers smeared with dirt. Either he had been sifting through someone's garbage can or digging up potatoes in some chump's allotment. More likely the former. Ray regarded him warily, skeptical about his motives. He was as appealing as the sighting of a rat in the bathroom in the middle of the night.

"I haven't eaten today," the man continued. "How about a small token of goodwill, buddy."

A kick to the backside was about all Ray wanted to spare him. The thought that he might scuff his shoe made him practice restraint.

"You look like a friendly guy. You have a bit o' cash you can spare for a starving man?"

The man certainly looked like a beggar, and he played the part well, but Ray had reservations about him. He had approached Ray too swiftly, intercepting him with measured care. There was something phony about his manner, a calculating glint in his eye.

Ray decided to play along. "Goodwill, huh. Sure. I think I have some loose change."

He reached into his pocket and rummaged around, rearranging the contents and surreptitiously trying not to inadvertently pull out some banknotes. His fingers finally closed around some coins, and as he withdrew his hand from his pocket, it was in the shape of a fist.

Nobody made any sudden moves, persuading Ray to loosen his fist. He opened his hand out thoroughly to reveal five coins in his palm. After shuffling them about a bit, he passed three coins to the man.

The cracked, darkly purple lips twisted into a distracting smile. "Thank you, friend."

The other man walking beside him was equally disheveled. There were rips in his unbuttoned coat and holes in the sweater he wore beneath. He hadn't shaved for months, maybe years, and the specks in his beard were probably just lint, but there was also a hint they might be moldy food particles.

Ray handed the man the remaining coins, and then he flinched when he felt the man's icy fingers make contact with his skin. The touch disgusted him, and he felt an impulse to run to a bathroom and scrub his hands with soap, possibly even bleach.

The man was large and stout, and he smelled like vinegar and curds. He was the epitome of a man who slept under the stars and bathed once a year, probably in a creek. His teeth were yellowish, what was left of them, and his lumpy red nose was too large for his face. He might have suffered from rhinophyma, or perhaps he was born that way.

Ray felt the man's cold fingers extend across his palm, latching around his hand with disturbing menace, and what started as a gentle touch quickly became a firm squeeze and then a vice-like grip. Ray stared at him anxiously, taking in the unsmiling eyes, unable to free his hand and alarmed at how his arm was being jerked up and down. There was strength in the action and rhythm, and Ray wasn't sure quite what to make of it other than the fact that this unkempt stranger was too strong and intimidating to be a common vagabond. There was nothing broken about him. He had the eyes of a felon and the bearing of a mobster. And that powerful grip...he could wrestle a bear with those hands!

Ray took a small step backward, trying to yank his arm free, but the man clasped it defiantly, preventing an escape. The guy was determined to make sure that Ray didn't go anywhere.

"Nice to meet you, buddy," he told Ray, grinning insanely and baring his teeth. They weren't just yellowish; there were gray ones, too, and a few black fillings. "Always nice to meet good people."

He continued to pull on Ray's arm as he chattered, perhaps seeing if he could jerk it out of the socket. It then occurred to Ray that he wasn't actually being assaulted. Not entirely. The man was shaking his hand, not attempting to dislocate his shoulder.

The sociable gesture was really quite monstrous. It was rash and gratuitous, and from Ray's perspective, most unwelcome, and he found himself muttering, "Better let go before this turns into tug-of-war."

"I could do with a smoke, as well," the man said gruffly, finally letting go of him. The raspy, splintered tone of his voice sounded like he routinely gargled with carpenter's nails. "Any chance you can spare us a couple cigs?"

Ray put his hand into his jacket pocket. As he flexed his fingers, they brushed against the switchblade. He watched the two men cautiously, contemplating if it was needed and calculating his chances if he decided to put it to use. *Later*, he thought, deciding it was a last resort. He still hoped he might be able to learn something valuable about the reverend and the iniquitous work he was conducting in a house of worship. The pocketknife would ruin those hopes.

His hand emerged from his pocket, holding a packet of Lucky Strikes. He flicked the bottom of the carton twice, causing two cigarettes to be elevated above the others. "Here you go," he said, offering them to the strangers.

"I haven't seen you around here before," croaked the bearded stranger, taking a cigarette. "You new in town?"

Ray nodded. "Got here yesterday."

The other stranger took a cigarette. "From where?"

"Chicago."

The bearded man took over again as if they were playing tag. "That's some move. What brings you here?"

So, this was how they dealt with newcomers, thought Ray, admiring the simplicity of Sinclair's vetting process. "I'm a salesman. My company transferred me here to develop a new client base. Thought it would be sensible to check out the neighborhood and meet with the local parishioners. I would also like to meet with the reverend. What time does he give his sermon?"

"He'll be thrilled to meet a new face. I'll take you to him."

Ray hesitated, but the man's strong hand clasped his shoulder and steered him away from the entrance.

"Where are we going?" Ray demanded. "The back door?"

"You'll find the minister around here," insisted the man.

"In the cemetery?" said Ray, doubtfully.

"Yes, this way," came the brusque response.

Ray felt the immediate threat of danger. He had failed some sort of initiation test and was now being denied access to the church and Sinclair. Was he being led to a place of reckoning for trying to gain admission under false pretenses? It seemed slightly ludicrous and hardly likely in a public space during daylight hours.

As he was jostled around the back of the church, he noticed several large trucks stationed in the parking lot. Two men in overalls were loading crates into the back of one of the vehicles. They paid Ray no attention.

"I'll see the pastor later. Let go of me, will you!" Ray demanded.

His immediate inclination was to run, but the other man sensed what he was about to do and blocked him with his body. Ray found himself sandwiched between the two, strongarmed toward the boneyard.

Ray elbowed one in the ribs and tried to wrench his arm free of the other, but he didn't manage to slip away in time. Each man got a good hold of his arms, dragging him the remaining distance, and then he was shoved unceremoniously at a rickety metal gate that gave way the instant he collided with it. He stumbled across the burial ground and fell face-first into the unmown grass in a footlong space between two gravestones. He heard the low whine of the gate being closed and the soft click as it was fastened shut.

The two men rushed at him as he scrambled to his feet. He barely had time to put up his arm to block the first punch, and the second fist caught him flush on his left cheek. As he staggered backward, trying to keep his footing, another whack to the head rattled his teeth. The world went into a slow spin, and his feet kept shifting around, struggling to find firm ground.

Before he had a chance to recover, a combination of punches to his chest and head dropped him onto his backside, and he sat there staring up at one of the thugs, seeing only too large fists full of rage and power. The jagged knuckles were ready for action and looked like they would do some damage.

Ray rolled in the dirt and managed to find his feet at last. His vision was blurry, his face throbbing with pain. It was a challenge knowing where to look; the two homeless bums had morphed into four mighty prizefighters keen to pummel him into oblivion.

He steadied himself and raised his fists, hoping they might do him proud. As one of the men rushed at him, Ray rather surprised himself by managing to dodge the man's slow hook and land a jab on the thug's thin jaw. Down he went, tipping sideways like a felled oak, hitting the ground with colossal force. Ray almost whooped for joy, delighted with his punch and pleased to hear his victim wheezing fitfully.

His joy was short-lived. The second man slammed into Ray, taking him down hard onto his back, making him moan and lament the painful landing. A split second later, his pain intensified as the full force of the man's knee came crashing down on his stomach. He growled in pain and tried to curl into a ball, but the man's energetic blows stopped him from getting into a protective pose.

As he was howling in distress, getting thoroughly pummeled between wails, he managed to swing a fist and clip the thug on the chin. The man lurched sideways, almost losing his balance completely, but he recovered in time and returned a decent wallop to Ray's abdomen. It felt like a hammer blow, stunning him into silence. The man followed it with a couple more rapid punches that proved just as effective, and then he drove his fist onto Ray's ribcage, eager to find a new area of the body to soften up.

Ray flipped onto his side, gasping for air, convinced the

man had just shattered his ribs. There was no opportunity for a moment's recovery. The sole of a size ten boot stamped on his head, imprinting an intricate pattern of indentations across the side of Ray's face. A second kick was looming, but he didn't manage to land it before Ray caught hold of his foot and shoved him away.

Ray started to wriggle away, but immediately, the fiend was on top of him, his large, meaty hands enveloping Ray's face, ramming his head into the ground. Ray fought for breath as a hand pressed against his nostrils, smothering him.

He was choked of voice, pinned into submission, persuaded that in a matter of minutes, he was about to become a corpse. His body would be six feet in the ground before it was even cold. There were dozens of graves around him, dozens of old bones beneath the earth, and his bones would be mingled with someone else's burial plot, with no marker to identify his remains, no inscription in stone to detail when and where he was born, or the date of his death. There would be no mourners, no eulogy, no monument to tell future generations that a man with his name and exact date of birth once walked the earth.

As the life drained out of him, he managed one last act of defiance. With all the strength left in him, he brought his knee up viciously, catching the man on top of him right between the thighs.

He heard the injured shriek and then a satisfying whimper. The man's grubby fingers slid off his face as he rolled off Ray. He thudded against the earth like a sack of potatoes, clutching his groin in silent agony.

Ray greedily filled his lungs, devouring the air like fine wine. Then he scrambled to his feet and stood there, weak and unsteady, not quite sure which way to run.

He was suddenly conscious of the distinctive, mechanical noise of a switchblade clicking open.

Seven

Ray caught a glimpse of the nine-inch knife as the man's hand flashed at his face. He hopped back, dodging the blade, and impulsively, he thrust his hand into his pocket in search of his own weapon. His fingers pressed against the switchblade, and a stab of exhilaration passed through him.

He steadied himself as the man shuffled toward him, the knife blade angled toward the ground as if the intent was to inflict downward strikes. Ray's fingers tightened on the handle of his pocketknife, his thumb poised over the automatic release button, yet he was reluctant to remove it from his pocket. Then he became aware of the other man in his blind spot, clambering to his feet, bristling with fury and seeking cruel vengeance. The man was straightening up and flexing his fists, poised to strike.

Ray took another step back, distracted by the second man's movements but trying not to take his eyes off the one with the switchblade. He knew the duo would attack in unison, one from behind with his fists while the other lunged with the knife, looking to cleave a pretty pattern across Ray's face. Two violent thugs posing as impoverished vagrants, preying on the goodwill of churchgoers. Of course, it was no coincidence that Ray had found them here, in this treacherous neighborhood. They were a crucial part of Arnold Sinclair's clan. His inconspicuous security force was ever ready to defend their master. Who would ever suspect that a posse of destitute hobos, swaddled in newspaper blankets on nearby public benches, were watchmen armed with knives and a boxer's savvy?

Yet, the extent of this vicious assault confounded Ray. Was the intention to scare him away, or was murder part of their list of crimes?

He retreated further as the two men inched closer, seemingly intending to corner him against the crumbling mausoleum ten feet away. He needed the protection of the switchblade in his pocket, but he feared the consequences of exposing it. Removing it now would be a declaration that Ray was more than simply a Chicago salesman innocently seeking to meet parishioners to find new clients. Evidently, he had aroused their suspicions and endangered his mission. It seemed inevitable that these men would inform Sinclair about him, probably making the reverend even more elusive and security conscious.

Ray released his grip on the switchblade and took his hand out of his pocket, deciding against utilizing his knife skills. It was a matter of fight or flight, and fortunately, he was blessed with speed and agility.

He turned and fled, sprinting around the back of the mausoleum and zigzagging between gravestones. He heard the brisk patter of feet close behind and kept his eyes trained ahead, focused on putting distance between himself and Sinclair's men.

As he made a beeline for the wall at the back of the cemetery, a slither of metal whizzed by his ear and clattered against the rutted stone. He glanced down, managing not to break stride, and saw a knife on the ground.

A second later, he made a frantic leap at the wall. His knees collided painfully against the stone, but he managed to secure a hold on the lip of the wall and find a solid foothold. He swung his agile body over in one fluid motion, dropping safely to the ground on the other side.

His thigh muscles throbbed as he landed. Despite the pain, he broke into a sprint, glancing back only once to make sure he wasn't being followed. He didn't stop until the church grounds were no longer visible.

When he returned to his hotel, he was angry and frustrated. He wanted to revisit Southie and find another way into the church. Sinclair's efforts to vet parishioners and discourage intruders made him wonder about the security measures deployed inside the church. Doubtless, the reverend had a backup plan for combatting those determined to find a way inside, and Ray figured there was a good alarm system in place. Likely, his treasures were contained in a strongroom that resembled a bank vault rather than a sacristy or a crypt. Ray pictured hidden compartments, reinforced walls, combination mechanisms, and time locks.

He never could resist a challenge. Picking locks was his specialty. The desire to test his skills made him plan a return visit in the morning. He would need an appropriate disguise. A gray wig, perhaps, and a furry white beard. Could he pull off dressing as a woman? He laughed as he imagined the costume: a shapeless dress, maybe a muumuu, and a bit of makeup on his face, smeared on like face paint, of course. Some padding in the right places.

He shuddered as he imagined his appearance. The idea of him in a dress was horrifying rather than comic.

The more he thought it over, the more foolish a return to the church seemed. Without question, he would jeopardize his chances of locating the necklace, and precisely what did he hope to achieve anyway? Was there any value in sitting on a wooden pew, trying to look pious? Would merely being in a drafty place of repose reveal anything significant to him or simply put him in harm's way?

Ray sat on the bed in his hotel room, apprehensive about his assignment. Through his visit to Southie, he had drawn unnecessary attention to himself, and from now on, he would need to be discreet.

His eyes surveyed his motel room as he strategized a new

course of action. His gaze stopped on the half-full Johnnie Walker Red Label bottle on the table. Automatically, he reached for it.

He drew his inspiration from a liquor bottle in much the same way a man of the cloth might with a bible, and thinking about the whiskey reminded him of Merriam. He wondered what she was doing now and how he might approach her.

He left the bottle of whiskey where it was and exited his room, going to the phone in the hotel lobby. He dropped a coin in the slot and dialed Walter's number. The phone rang for a long time, but he didn't hang up. He gazed at the wall distractedly as he waited, focusing on a bug. At first, he thought it might be a cockroach. Len's remark about the cleanliness of the Slate Gray Motor Hotel continued to play on his mind, and no matter that the Hotel Buckminster was vastly superior, he couldn't get the idea of cockroaches out of his head. He stared hard at the insect, trying to determine the species. It was approximately one inch in length and a dull brown color. The sight of it unnerved him slightly, but he felt an immediate sense of relief when he realized it was nothing more sinister than a field cricket.

The phone stopped ringing, and a gravelly voice growled into the receiver, "*Ja? Wer ist das?*"

For a brief moment, he thought he had misdialed. As he was about to hang up, he remembered Günter, Walter's insolent new hire. The irritating sound of Günter's voice made Ray hiss into the mouthpiece, "In English, you jackass!"

"*Ja*, of course. I forget. Who's speaking?"

"Ray Stokes. Where's Walter?"

"Stokes!" Günter said his name with distaste. Somehow, he managed to sound out the name like it was a diseased maggot.

"Just get me Walter," Ray said impatiently.

"I don't like how you speak to me," responded Günter. "You have no manners."

"Never mind that," grumbled Ray. "Is Walter home or not? If he is, put him on."

"He's not available. His Swedish masseuse hasn't finished with him yet."

"A massage! Interrupt him, dammit!"

The rich man's idyllic life appalled him. Apparently, Walter's hectic social calendar and those stressful auctions necessitated daily Swedish massages. Ray could imagine the sort of rubdown his boss was getting. Of course, it had nothing to do with him needing to unwind after a stressful day of cataloging artifacts and everything to do with him wanting to encourage the muscles to come to life after long periods of inactivity.

"He gave explicit instructions he shouldn't be disturbed," Günter argued.

"I can't feed this telephone all day. I don't have the time or the coins. Tell him to keep his Swede on ice until later."

"I'll get him, but he won't be happy."

Ray absently played with a nickel. It traveled between his fingers with speed. It was the only party trick he knew, and he practiced it often. The coin would flip from knuckle to knuckle, frequently without him being aware of what he was doing. His fast hands were like a magician, and he could make the coin magically disappear at will like Walter could make a person disappear whenever he wanted.

Ray was down to his last nickel when the old man finally came to the phone.

"Any news, Ray? You must be in Boston by now," he said, sounding tired and wheezy.

Ray talked hurriedly, concerned that the call might drop. "Yes, I'm in Boston. I've seen Sinclair's church. It's a hive of activity. He's got guards on the front entrance posing as bums."

"Did you scope the inside?"

"No. No chance yet."

"Then leave it alone," Walter insisted. "Remember, Merriam is the key. That's why you're in Boston. Stick to the plan. Make contact with her. Try to build up a rapport. She's our best chance of getting the necklace."

"Perhaps," said Ray, still unsure about Walter's plan. "Sinclair is vetting newcomers, but parishioners come and go all the while. We just need to get a man inside the building. With a bit of time, I'm sure we can break into whatever room or vault Sinclair is storing his valuables."

"Leave the church alone, Ray. I'll send a surveillance team out tomorrow to find ways to gain access."

"It will take time to build a relationship with Merriam."

"Work fast, Ray. I've found that relationships move quickly in the beginning. A friendship, a romance, they begin suddenly and progress at a remarkable rate," maintained Walter, sounding like an authority on the subject. "After a year or less, a marriage grows stale. But a new and exciting stranger can make a powerful impact. Seize her, shake her up, make her giddy with desire."

Ray put a hand to his face and massaged his eyes. Walter seemed to be under the impression he was some sort of aphrodisiac, that he could charm a pretty dame from across a busy street.

"I can't work miracles, Walter. Perhaps the reverend can, but not me. If I try to force a casual encounter into something more meaningful, she'll see through it."

Walter chuckled dismissively. "A man with your guile and charisma can have Merriam swooning into your arms with just a gentle touch."

"Christ!" Ray muttered, perturbed by Walter's ridiculously high opinion of him. "She'll see me coming a mile off and be hiding behind Sinclair's pulpit robe in five minutes flat."

"Merriam will be putty in your hands, I know it," Walter said, utterly convinced. "The girl will be murmuring sweet endearments in your ear after ten minutes in your company. Heck, she'll be sending out wedding invitations after an hour."

When Ray replaced the telephone receiver, his face was etched with worry lines. A regular girl in a dancehall looking for a companion was one thing, but seducing another man's mistress to extract information was something else entirely. Frankly, he didn't feel up to the task.

He looked up at the ceiling disconsolately and said a little prayer.

————— ✦ —————

There were two types of women who were typically attracted to Ray Stokes: naive young hopefuls looking for a potential husband and man-hungry vixens looking for amorous escapades. Ray couldn't handle either one for any extended length of time. He was a womanizer who liked to be in complete control. At this stage in his life, he had no desire to burden himself with a joy-sucking ball and chain forever in his home, nagging and demanding things of him, exhausting his bank account, and finding ways to spoil his day.

Merriam Woodcroft seemed very different from the women Ray was accustomed to. There was a frostiness about her that was in sharp contrast to the summer heat in Boston. As Ray rode the streetcar with her in the morning, he surreptitiously scrutinized her, hoping to glean something about her that might serve him later. She wore a brush stroke print dress with a finely pebbled texture that seemed to cling to her contours. The shoulder drapery highlighted her smooth, milky white neckline. A simple gold necklace drooped around her slender neck.

He admired her easy elegance and her appealing silhouette. In fact, he found himself dabbing his mouth with a pocket handkerchief, convinced that he was drooling.

She wasn't aware that he was gawping at her. She was engrossed in a book and unwilling to look up from her page, even when passengers filed in and out of the streetcar. *Must be one hell of a book*, he thought.

When the streetcar came to a brief stop at Back Bay station, he moved from the back of the compartment and filtered into the crowd of newcomers, forcing his way next to Merriam. He leaned over and glimpsed the title of the book she was reading: *Peyton Place* by Grace Metalious.

Ray ran a finger across his chin, lost in thought. If his memory served him correctly, it was a book about three females: a mother, her illegitimate daughter, and a working-class woman from the slums. They all had skeletons in their closets that they were trying desperately to hide. What were those secrets? Extramarital sex, incest, pregnancy, abortion, and murder. A small-town peep show, indeed. It was little wonder Merriam was so thoroughly immersed in it.

"Steamy goings-on in prim New England," he said in a breathy whisper, his lips intimately close to her earlobe.

She exhibited a discomfited shiver but didn't look at him.

He went on undeterred. "What exactly is buried in the sheep pen in the Cross's yard?"

She finally made eye contact with him. Her face didn't carry the inquiring look he had been anticipating; in fact, she was glaring at him.

"Excuse me, I'm trying to read," she said sternly. "Could you please not stand so close."

He apologized and moved back fractionally. "Is that better?"

"Not really." There was exasperation in her eyes. "Would you mind turning your face the other way? I get claustrophobic, and with you leaning over me like this, I feel as if you're practically on top of me."

"Forgive me. These cars get so crowded."

Her gaze returned to the book in her hands. She quickly picked up where she had left off and rapidly turned the page.

He shrugged with indifference, unperturbed by her chilly response, and peered out of the window through the cluster of heads around him. There was nothing much to see beyond gray skies and glimpses of drab buildings. He noticed they were approaching Chinatown.

When he looked back at Merriam, intending to engage her in further conversation, she sensed his eyes boring into her and angled her book so that it was directly in front of his face, obstructing his view.

He cupped his hand to his nose and mouth and breathed into it, trying to ascertain the state of his breath. It smelled okay, as far as he could tell, so he leaned in again, about to open a new topic of conversation.

The book's spine suddenly came down on the bridge of his nose, causing him to let out a faint moan.

Merriam didn't appear to be aware of her carelessness with the book.

He wanted to grab the book and throw it on the floor. Somehow, he managed to keep his emotions in check.

Seconds later, the streetcar came to another brief stop, and a flurry of passengers exited the vehicle. Before others could board, Merriam seized the opportunity to reposition herself in a different part of the car, well away from Ray.

He sank back into a throng of people and stared vacantly at the back of a fat man in front of him. He needed time to put his wretched first encounter with Merriam behind him.

———◆———

Ray continued to ride the same streetcar as Merriam in the mornings and the evenings, tailing her to and from the Holy Trinity church. Hopeful, at first, gradually, he came to consider the journeys to be a futile exercise. The more he studied her, the more he began to think of her as an emotionless, mechanical toy. She was unconventional, clean, tidy, and lacking spontaneity, devoid of interesting characteristics. She rarely looked up from her book and refrained from eye contact in the street. When not in Sinclair's company, she seemed cold and aloof, disinterested in men. She was also maddeningly punctual, rarely varying her routine. She left her home at the same time each day, arriving at work early. She rode the same streetcars to and from work. She ate and slept at the same time each day. Ray suspected she had bowel movements at precisely the same time every day, and maybe the consistency of her stools didn't vary either.

She seemed as stiff and humorless as a Swiss bank clerk, making him believe she must be the same way in the workplace. Efficient, disciplined, organized, boring.

Though her monotonous routine didn't fluctuate, her daily change of outfit didn't fail to captivate him. She must have had a gargantuan walk-in closet full of the most luxurious fashions, and everything she wore looked like it had been designed specifically to accommodate her sublime measurements. Her turquoise blue whirl skirt didn't appear out of place on her journey to work. The next day, when he saw her in a gold, white, and black striped Ivy League shirt, he could scarcely take his eyes off her. One day, she sported a wool tweed sweater skirt with multi-color flecks. It had a button-tab trim and side kick pleat, and such fine tailoring that Ray wondered about her finances. Her quality clothes were never shabby, and they always fitted her pleasingly. She was a woman made to stand out in a crowd, no matter how dour her expression.

One evening, as she moved to the streetcar doors, preparing to get off, Ray made another forceful effort to engage her in conversation. He moved close behind her, keeping his head averted, knowing he had to draw her attention artfully. Right then, the worst thing to do was to get too close and make her feel claustrophobic again. The feel of his breath on her neck might set her off and make her pound him on the nose again with her book.

When she started down the steps, he accidentally banged her on the hip with his briefcase. She spilled out of the streetcar, staggering foolishly on the sidewalk, arms swinging in roundhouse style. He scrambled down the steps after her, thinking she would fall, determined to catch her. Somehow, she managed to stay on her feet.

He apologized profusely, but it didn't do much good. Merriam turned to him with a look of fury and jabbed him in the chest with her index finger. Her sharp nail pressed painfully against him, leaving an impression on the skin. "You utter oaf!" she raged. "I hope you fall down a large stairway and break your leg someday."

It was a gloriously mean remark that had the sort of sting a slap on the butt cheek with a twisted damp towel might achieve. Ray was embarrassed by the tongue-lashing, but he took heart from the fact he had inadvertently produced a strong emotional response from her.

She glanced down at his handsome tan cowhide briefcase and chided him for mishandling such attractive hand luggage. "You should be more careful," she said, examining it keenly. "You might have scuffed it on the door of the tram."

"You're right," he agreed, petting the briefcase affectionately.

"And thanks for trying to catch me," she added. "You're an oaf, but at least you're considerate."

He stared wide-eyed, surprised by her unexpected gratitude. The hard edges were momentarily gone, and there was gentleness and warmth in her face.

She noticed his bottom jaw drop and smirked, commenting: "I like that look. It's like a deer caught in headlights."

He nodded again, thinking: *Damn, she's beautiful.*

"What's the matter?" she pressed. "Seen a ghost?"

"An angel, more like," he muttered freely.

The compliment rammed her like a bumper car. "Oh, that's good," she said with amusement.

The streetcar began to pull away, leaving them alone on the street corner.

"Your smile is delightful," he explained. "It's the first time I've seen it. It took me by surprise."

"You've no fear about speaking your mind," she observed. "See something you like, and you go straight for it."

"I'm not usually so forward," he admitted.

"Doubt that," she said, contesting the sincerity of his words. "A face like yours wins admirers easily. I imagine you're very popular with the ladies."

"Hardly," he said dismissively. "Would it be too forward if I suggested we go for a drink?"

"Yes."

He shrugged off the rebuff. "How about I walk you home?"

She glanced around as if suddenly concerned someone might see her talking to him. Seeing nobody, she said, "Very well. I don't live far from here."

As they walked side by side, he casually remarked, "I see you on the streetcar each day. You always have your head in a book."

"I like to read," she admitted defensively.

"Fiction?"

"Yes, fiction. Don't you read?"

"Yes, I read. Not fiction, though. Newspapers. I like real events."

She prickled at the remark. "The creative element is always present in news stories. Statistics get twisted. Opinions are dressed up as fact."

"Oh yes?" he muttered, encouraging her to say more.

"World events are heightened to seem more interesting than they really are," she continued. "Take the Far East flu, for example. Now it's reached the United States, newsmen are bloating the story out of all proportions."

"You're saying the numbers are inflated? You don't think it's as deadly as they say?"

"What are we up to now? Twenty-five thousand cases. Twenty thousand in San Diego alone. I read one column the other day that this winter, once the cold weather hits, we can expect thirty-four million Americans to catch the virus."

"Scaremongering. That what you think?"

"Of course. And they're pushing a vaccine that's seventy percent effective, hoping for sixty million Americans to get it by February first. They're focusing on this mutant strain like it's more deadly than the Spanish flu. It's a neat way to revitalize factories and maintain a thriving workforce, isn't it?"

Ray shrugged and looked a little confused.

"And then there's all that misinformation and the deliberate misquotations. Details manipulated to serve political agendas. Deception as strategy in times of war is one thing, but purposeful efforts to discredit a person or organization, or just plain cloud an issue for party-political ends, well, it's a long walk from freedom and liberty, isn't it?"

Ray started to nod his head but realized he didn't fully comprehend her perspective. She clearly had an axe to grind.

"*Maskirovka* is a Russian term meaning masking. A military phrase for camouflage. The end of World War II didn't stop our major newspapers from their smoke and mirrors on the battlefield methods. They've always sought to influence perceptions and behaviors, but their deceptive, biased reporting is too much. It's a propaganda tool, no different from Soviet tricks to control its people. At the moment, the *New York Times* has a correspondent promoting Castro and his revolutionaries. He's just got back from the Sierra Maestro mountains where he was palling around with this rebel leader of Cuba's youth, sleeping under the stars, oiling the man's gun barrel and whatnot. Now the *New York Times* is printing the interviews, publicizing Castro and his campaign promises, tenaciously circulating his manifesto."

"I quite like the *New York Times*," he said with a shrug. "That's the stuff I like to read. Fiction masquerading as fact, with some good old journalistic flair."

"You mean stuff spewed out by some half-pickled hack who flunked English in high school?"

He rolled his eyes. "Have you ever read the *Boston Globe*? I'd hardly call their writers high school dropouts."

"Oh, the *Boston Globe*, yes, of course," she said contritely. "I didn't realize you were talking about those trusted scribes. Noble world commentators with PhDs in being fair and balanced."

He scratched his head, wondering how the conversation had become political.

She quickened her pace, moving ahead of him, making him lengthen his stride to catch up. He matched her pace, and then she suddenly stopped and said, "Listen, I'm okay walking by myself. I'm sure you have other things you ought to be doing."

"It's fine."

"It isn't. You should go."

He had expected resistance, and he was determined to prevail. "I'd like to walk you home."

"Why?" she asked skeptically.

"I enjoy your company. I'd like to get to know you."

"Why?" she asked again, with growing suspicion.

"I see you on the train each day, and I find myself drawn to you. Now I learn you're a woman with strong opinions, and I'm intrigued to hear more of them."

"What I see is a man desperately wanting something that doesn't exist," she bluntly said. "I'm no different from a thousand others who walk up and down this street every day. If you look more closely, you'll see I'm not what you want or need."

"Let me be the judge."

"Why waste your time?"

"It's mine to waste," he protested. "Let me walk you to your door."

"I'd rather you didn't. You seem like a lovely man. A charmer. But I'm simply not interested. I have enough friends in my life."

"You can never have too many friends."

"I believe you can. I'll see you on the train tomorrow, I'm sure."

His eyes followed her as she walked down the street, enjoying the enticing wiggle in her hips. He wondered about the reverend and the man's capacity to charm. A Higher Power was a work here, Ray realized. There was no other explanation for it. Sinclair must have sold his soul to the devil, and that heinous force was raising the conman to ludicrous heights. The beautiful mistress, the church vault full of lost treasures, the endless supply of money and merchandise and willing buyers…the pastor's journey to magnificent riches and pleasures of the flesh was absurd. It stank.

A look at Merriam's shapely legs made Ray want to steal the gold-platted fountain pen from the devil's top pocket and ink his grandiose signature on the gnarly bit of parchment the old rogue was toting. *Just shove the paperwork in my clammy hand*, thought Ray, *and I'll sign the damn thing in blood.*

Eight

A couple of days later, while Ray was riding the streetcar, feigning interest in a book he regretted purchasing at a newsstand, he thought he saw Merriam smiling at him. It was a faint, coy smile that was at odds with her usual somber countenance.

When the streetcar reached Merriam's stop, Ray hurried through the car, offering insincere apologies as he elbowed past the tightly packed passengers. Merriam briefly disappeared in the crowd, and when the vehicle came to a jerky stop and the doors rattled open, he found himself toward the front of the line. He looked around but didn't see Merriam, and then he was jostled down the steps.

He felt the hard heel of someone's hand thumping into him, prodding him in the small of the back. His hand slid off the stair rail, and his foot missed the next step. With a frightened gasp, he plunged out of the streetcar.

As he fell, face first, he suffered a ghastly little scare that raised the hair on the back of his neck and ratcheted up his heart rate. His palms slapped against the sidewalk, protecting the rest of him from injury, and his sparkling new chestnut Wingtip Oxfords clanked loudly on the ground, signaling the completion of his emphatic tumble.

He lifted his head and gazed at the passersby, wondering what kind of spectacle he had made of himself. To those nearby, the clatter of his shoes sounded like horse's hooves, and several pedestrians abruptly altered their path, regarding him as a dangerous lunatic who was either under the influence of a powerful narcotic or simply soft in the head. At any rate, they avoided eye contact with him, giving him a wide berth.

He rose to his feet and surveyed the doorway of the tram, keen to see who had shoved him in the back. Merriam carefully made her way down the steps, the guilty smile identifying her as the culprit.

"You pushed me," he said bitterly.

"Did I?" Her cool detachment convinced him she was unrepentant. To cap it off, there was an unmistakable gleam of satisfaction in her eyes.

"You know damn well you did."

"I was trying to get your attention," she explained.

"By pushing me down the stairs?"

"Is that what you think? What a low opinion you must have of me."

"It was a push. You think I don't know the difference between a pat on the shoulder and a shove in the back? You could have seriously hurt me."

The hostility in his eyes caused the twinkle in her eyes to wane. "Yes, I understand your concern," she conceded solemnly. "You might have grazed your lips or bruised your nose. And where would you be if someone spoiled your looks?"

He heard the doors to the streetcar snap shut, and then the vehicle began to pull away.

Merriam started to walk, but he planted his feet in front of her, bringing her to a halt.

"You said you wanted to get my attention. Well? What did you want to say?"

She shrugged and let a couple of frown lines tarnish her smooth forehead. "I was curious about your book," she said.

He shook his head. "Book?"

"I saw you reading a book in the streetcar."

He had no recollection of reading anything other than street signs.

She pointed to the book sticking out of his jacket pocket. He noticed it, as if for the first time, and pulled it out to see exactly what it might be.

"*The Wounded and the Slain*," she said, reading the title aloud. "It's a novel, isn't it? That's interesting. I thought you didn't read novels. You said you preferred newspapers. Real events."

He looked at the book with remorse. "That's right. I can't remember the last time I picked up a novel. Your comments the other day persuaded me to take another stab at fiction."

"And of all the novels, you chose this one. Any particular reason?"

"Must there be a reason?"

She gave him a condescending look. "Of course there must."

"I saw it at the newsstand. It jumped out at me."

She nodded. "Those Gold Medal covers have a habit of doing that. What's this book about? Is it any good?"

He gazed at the cover, flipped it over, and began silently reading the blurb on the back. He hadn't read much of the book, and for the life of him, he couldn't recall the plot or even the characters.

She peered at the book a little closer. "David Goodis. He's that depressing writer of suspense novels, isn't he? Tragic and melancholic, likes to plunge the reader into the murky shadows of human misery."

Ray nodded vacantly, angling for an opportunity to steer the conversation elsewhere.

"He's not dissimilar to Cornell Woolrich. Obviously, he's a hugely talented writer: complex and analytical. Yet Goodis doesn't so much write crime tales as present intense psychological studies of losers and victims and thoroughly rotten people. They tend to be tormented and desperately lost; pitiful wretches who are out of their depth, floundering in deep, murky waters, so to speak, and scrambling steadily toward further pain and despair."

Ray grunted uninterestedly, but she was on a roll, and there was no stopping her.

"You get the feeling when you read his work that his protagonists are like diseased creatures experiencing a long and painful death. They are born to suffer, and there is never any hint that their luck might change."

Ray glanced again at the book. The cover, he noticed, was slightly smeared, and the book felt unusually heavy. More like a brick than a paperback. He no longer had any desire to continue reading it. In fact, Merriam had put him off attempting any more of the author's work.

"I'm curious what you will make of the story when you're finished with it," she said, making him feel embarrassed about wanting to get shot of the book. "Perhaps you will love it, talk of it glowingly, and inspire me to read it. I might be compelled to re-evaluate the author."

"Yes, perhaps," muttered Ray, somberly.

He didn't feel obliged to read another page and had no intention of opening the book. If there were ever to be another conversation with Merriam, he would make damn sure that neither Goodis nor this book was ever discussed again.

"Well, I had better be going," she announced, moving past him. "Goodbye."

"Wait," he insisted. "Let's talk more. Care to join me for a drink at the Baker's Arms?"

"I can't. I'm working tonight."

"I thought you'd finished work and were going home," he blurted out.

"I waitress occasionally; tonight, I must cover for a friend."

"Where?"

"Don's Cookroom. Listen, sorry about accidentally pushing you down the stairs. I'm glad your face isn't ruined."

He watched her head down the street, wondering if he was like one of those pitiful, tormented wretches Goodis liked to write about. The fact she had a waitressing job tonight made him hope his luck was about to change.

He started down the street in the opposite direction, stopping at the nearest trashcan. With a heavy sigh, he tossed the book into it.

———— ✦ ————

Ray sat on the edge of the bed in his hotel room, slouched forward with his head in his hands. While it appeared as if he was in the throes of suffering and agitation, this was, in fact, his reflective pose. The suffering and agitation would come later.

He quietly mulled over his conversation with Merriam some hours earlier, feeling positive about the outcome. He genuinely didn't care if he appealed to her or not. She was a job, nothing more. There was a faint sense of dread, though, that he couldn't dispel. Rather than a challenge, he regarded her as a potential fiasco. Ultimately, a perceived lack of success would undermine his relationship with Walter, diminishing his value.

The man truly believed that Ray had special powers over women. Where Medusa could turn to stone those who gazed upon her face, it was Walter's belief that Ray could melt a girl's heart at twenty paces.

Ray understood his strengths and weaknesses and knew what others envied in him. What he had, as far as his primary strengths, was his beguiling beauty and the continual blessings of Dame Fortune. As Walter had rightly noted, women typically fell for Ray—some harder than others—but what the old man didn't know was that for all the notches on Ray's bedpost, there were quite a few misses. Alas, women could be fickle creatures, and Ray had been snubbed and discarded by the best of them. Not that he cared. He changed partners almost as frequently as he changed his fancy outfits, gathering arm candy much like a Turkish sultan amassed concubines. He liked variety and diversity, but unlike the sultan, Ray had no interest in accumulating four wives, purely one-time playthings.

He had been told often enough that he lacked self-control, that he was unable to resist a pretty girl. The verdict was that he was a perpetual philanderer, unwilling to get emotionally involved. Consequently, he bore sadness and heartbreak, leaving some young women pining for his return.

His view was that nobody truly satisfied him, so none of his romances lasted beyond a week. It was unlikely that he would change anytime soon.

Cool as ice and resistant to his charms, Merriam might yet thaw a little if he persisted in his attempts to forge a relationship with her. Whether she would soften enough toward him to be as pliant as he needed her to be was another matter entirely. Exactly how to win her confidence was a puzzle he didn't have the time or the patience to strategize over. What he really needed was for the reverend to have a change of heart, vowing to be a faithful, loving husband and father and unselfishly casting aside his mistress. Of course, that sort of turnaround would require a miracle from above. Better odds were that Sinclair would walk on water.

Ray got up from the bed and paced around the room like a demented patrol guard. He had a sudden craving for buttered scones. Over the past couple of weeks, he had developed an unhealthy lifestyle, and the bad diet and prolonged periods of inactivity were sabotaging his lean, muscular figure.

He grabbed his jacket off the back of the chair and wrestled his arms into it. It was a gray flap pocket sport coat made of wool and silk. The coat had a nice, striped pattern that went well with his gabardine slacks. Only, it didn't button quite as tidily as it had the month before. In fact, it seemed to have shrunk a little, hugging his body more tightly. All the same, it didn't stop him from hungering for those buttered scones.

He exited his room and went down the stairs to the ground floor. As he stepped across the charming, circular lobby, he paused by a thick marble column near the main doors, wondering if he should stop at the bank of telephones and give Walter a progress update.

His lack of progress persuaded him to skip the phones and head for the door.

He caught the subway at Fenmore and got off at Arlington. A bus showed up within minutes, and he took it to West Broadway.

Dan's Cookroom was a short walk away and easy to locate. It lacked cleanliness and sophistication, but it was softly lit and had plenty of nicely furnished booths. He sat at an empty booth and waited for Merriam Woodcroft to come by his table. He was salivating by the time she finally approached him.

"What a surprise to see you here," she lied. "I didn't expect you to drop by tonight."

"Can't resist discovering new eateries in the area."

"What do you think of the place? Has its charm rubbed off on you yet?"

Ray examined the black smudge on the elbow of his jacket. "Some of it has left a mark."

She leaned in and said conspiratorially, "There's a better place down the street. CJ's kitchen. Serves great meatloaf."

"Not a fan of meatloaf," he told her. "But I might poke my head in later."

She pulled a notepad and pencil from her apron and nodded toward the table menu. "Made up your mind what you want?"

"Bacon, poached eggs, buttered toast, coffee," he said before she had an opportunity to list off the specials.

"Impressive," she responded. "Your tongue managed to scramble the bacon, bread, and eggs into one long word, and you disposed of two syllables somewhere along the way."

He gave an apologetic shrug. "There's me thinking that if I said it quickly, you would pass my order to the kitchen much faster."

The faint sounds emanating from his stomach indicated how hungry he was.

She scribbled in her little notepad. The words were indecipherable.

Without looking up, she said, "I see you so often that I feel like I know you already."

"We've barely scratched the surface," he disagreed. "We only really know each other's reading habits."

She squinted at him, a little frown taking root. "What is that, a Chicago accent?"

"Impressive," he said, mimicking her. "What gave me away?"

She shrugged. "It's a strong accent, and I thought I detected a faint variation in some of the vowel sounds."

"You a linguist on the side?"

"I like practicing different accents. I belong to an amateur dramatics society."

"I have an appreciation of the arts myself," he said as she moved to leave.

As he watched her tear off the sheet from her notepad and give it to the kitchen, he thought about a Bikini-clad burlesque dancer he had seen at the Tivoli Theatre in Mexico City a few years earlier. Now, there was a club where the performers were worth their salt, and that spirited redhead was the best by far. Her loose-limbed leopard dance made the mind boggle.

Ray took off his jacket, folded it neatly, and placed it on the seat beside him. Then he glanced at his watch to see how he was doing for time. It was now almost half past eight. He had gone without food a little too long and could feel a headache coming on.

Merriam returned with a coffee decanter and a platter containing a cup, utensils, and little pots of cream and sugar. "Are you working in Boston or visiting?"

"Just passing through, really. The boss is looking to expand his business. I'm here to foster sales in parts of Massachusetts."

She placed the tray on the table and set the cup in front of Ray. "How's it going so far?"

"Very slow. At this rate, I'll be here years."

As she leaned over to fill his cup with coffee, he looked admiringly at her shapely body, thinking how splendidly she filled out her uniform. She was wasted on a venue like Don's Cookroom. At the Tivoli Theatre, on the other hand, her physical assets would be put to far better use.

She finished pouring the coffee. "You need anything else?" she asked, preparing to move to another table.

"Perhaps later," he told her. "What time do you finish?"

She gazed at him uncertainly. "My shift ends at ten."

"You don't have long to go, then. Maybe we can grab some drinks nearby if you're not too tired."

Her hand quivered, causing the hot liquid to slosh around in the decanter.

"I'm not that the type of girl," she said indignantly.

"What type would that be?"

"An easy pick-up," she replied in a scolding tone.

"I didn't mean to offend. My intentions are honorable."

"Go on?" she encouraged, enticing the salesman's pitch.

"I've been on the telephone all day, flogging services nobody wants. I just want a relaxing evening with some pleasant company. It's been a while since I spent time in the company of a beautiful woman," he told her, believing a couple of weeks to be a long time.

"What's kept you from going on dates? Prison?"

"Just busy with work. Sales."

"Door-to-door, I suppose."

A raised voice at the other end of the diner drew her away, and his hungry eyes relished the smooth contours of her ample rear as she made her way to a corner table.

He sweetened his coffee with two spoonfuls of sugar and lightened it with cream. The coffee smelled good, and he devoured it greedily. As he idly rearranged the things on his table, he thought about his chances of locating the fantastic necklace that adorned Merriam's swanlike neck on special, sordid occasions. The odds of finding it didn't seem good.

Supposing, after four or five tireless weeks of tailing her, he had nothing to show for his efforts? Generally speaking, Ray had always managed to please his boss, but this was one of the few occasions where he felt it might have been better if he had turned the job down.

When Merriam returned with his food, she was quiet and chilly, making Ray believe that his charm had become as dry as the fried bacon on his plate. Walter's faith in him was misplaced.

"I'll come back with the change," she said, having returned with the check.

"No need," said Ray as she was about to head for the cash register.

"Thank you," she said, genuinely touched by his overgenerous tip.

He collected his coat from the seat, and as he rose from his chair, he muttered, "I can't imagine a better way to spend my evening. Your company is worth every penny."

She studied him quietly, her fingers absently fondling the twenty-dollar tip. Suddenly, she softened toward him. "You still interested in taking me out tonight?"

Nine

L ater, as they sat at a table in a chic cocktail lounge at the
ultra-modern club Jekyll's Fizz, Ray asked Merriam about
her waitressing work. He was curious if she had met Sinclair
while waiting tables in Don's Cookroom.

"I don't waitress often if that's what you're asking. Two or three
times a month at most. I cover shifts for my girl friend, Hen.
Waitressing isn't my favorite type of work," Merriam admitted.

"Too much of the wrong kind of attention from customers.
That is?"

"No, not really. Some of the customers can be quite interesting.
I just don't like to be on my feet all the time. I don't know how
Hen does it. My feet hurt like hell."

He nodded sympathetically. She was the type of woman who
would make a good living lying on her back.

"What other work do you do? In the daytime, that is?"

"I work as a secretary."

"Full time?"

She nodded.

"What sort of secretarial work do you do?" he asked, stifling
a yawn. "Not a legal secretary, are you?"

"I'm a financial secretary. I work in a church."

"Documenting collections and monetary gifts? Doing
monthly reports? That sort of thing?"

"Yes, that sort of thing."

"What are the challenges?" he pressed, desperate to learn some tasty tidbit. "Do you enjoy it?"

"There are lots of deposits and expenditures to track. The amount of paperwork would surprise you. The treasurer delegates the majority of the financial reporting to me, so I'm swamped each day. I do enjoy it, though."

"Lots of fundraising, I suppose. Are we talking big money?"

He observed a faint muscle spasm in her left cheek. Although hardly perceptible and otherwise not worth noting, he regarded this involuntary micro-expression as a sign of fear. There were details she didn't want to share, and yet, through nonverbal communication, she unwillingly leaked all manner of information. Decoding the signs in her expressions was his only key to determining the truth behind her words.

"You're not from the IRS, are you? I feel like you might be an undercover auditor."

He gave a fraudulent chuckle. Though sharp-eyed when it came to body language, he was incapable of masking his own attempts at deceit. "Sounds like you have a guilty conscience. All those church raffles and donation drives must amount to a pretty penny. Containers of cash to keep an eye on, huh? And there's probably page after page of dubious expenses. Creatively cataloging charges isn't easy."

"The pastor is very honorable," she said defensively, startled by his unexpected allegations. "A wonderful man, actually. Everything's above board."

"You hear such terrible stories about clergymen these days, don't you?" he continued with a little shake of his head. "Undocumented sex crimes and financial wrongdoings; seedy practices that go on for decades that the archbishop never condemns."

She watched him intently, displeased by his remarks. "We're all sinners. I'm sure if we draw back the curtains on your armoire, not everything will be clean and respectable."

"It's a fair comment. There are skeletons in my closet, for sure, but no blood stains."

"The red stains are there throughout the entire closet," she insisted sternly. "If you look closely."

The conviction in her voice unnerved him, and he began to wonder exactly how much she knew about him. All this time, he had misguidedly assumed that his real identity was carefully concealed and his employment untraceable. Now, he began to believe he was badly mistaken.

He stretched out his long legs under the table. The soft lighting and comfortable plush seating helped with his attempts to sedate his unease. The sudden presence of a waiter eager to take his order was even more helpful.

"Another Tom Collins," he told the man, believing one more drink would tranquilize those undermining fears.

"And for the lady?" the waiter asked. The man's gaze never once strayed from Merriam's face.

"The pink squirrel," she said.

The waiter smiled warmly and retreated. Ray tried not to read too much into the look.

"I'm not familiar with the drink you ordered," he told Merriam.

"It's not a new concoction. It's been around for more than a decade, actually. They say it originated in a cocktail lounge in Milwaukee. You should try it," she suggested.

He idly surveyed the hip venue, which was full of comfortable couches and patterned wallpaper. The showy, purple velvet curtains were perhaps an unnecessary extravagance. Whether they steered Jekyll's Fizz into the wrong era or added dramatic oldfangled ambiance, he couldn't quite tell.

"Fabulously eclectic establishment," he casually observed. "Every time I look around, I see something I hadn't previously noticed."

"Yes, isn't it fantastic? Crammed with fine-looking things,

don't you think? And not at all pretentious. I'd come here all the time if I could."

"What's stopping you?"

"My work gets in the way."

"After-hours work?"

She nodded.

"You mean bible studies and fellowship events?"

A shake of the head now. "Meetings and help with inventory."

"I take it the church thrives on bountiful donations?"

A further, more pronounced facial tremble presented itself. The muscle spasm confirmed Ray's suspicions about the inordinate traffic in and out of the parking lot behind the church. Purloined treasure staged to look like donated gifts, turning the church into a twenty-four-hour distribution center, successfully trafficking valuable contraband.

"It does okay," Merriam said blandly.

"Yet it keeps you incredibly busy. Maybe the church needs to hire more staff."

"They need more resources, but you know how it is with faith-based groups. They get by on volunteers and helpful companies offering in-kind help with services."

It was an interesting way of putting it. Ray could appreciate the difficulty for Sinclair. Greed brought an endless supply of merchandise to his carefully controlled facility, but issues of trust and discretion impacted his operation. The risks involved in expanding his small workforce were too great.

"It's a wonder you found time to escape the vestry," he said. "I'm fortunate to have met you on your night off."

"Yes," she agreed. "And I'd prefer not to discuss work on my night off."

He tried not to show his disappointment. The need to glean more information was strong; it felt like he had only touched the surface of her daily routine.

He swiftly changed topics, asking her about her local amateur dramatics society. Typically, it was a subject that interested him very little, but as Merriam discussed various productions and venues and anecdotes about disastrous rehearsals and problematic fellow performers, he became fascinated by her experiences, vowing to catch one of her future performances.

"What's the next play your company is doing?" he asked.

"*The Man Who Came to Dinner.*"

The answer surprised him. He had seen it performed once before on the West Coast. The drama critic Alexander Woollcott had played the lead, which was pleasing, given that the part was written specifically for him. Woollcott had turned down the Broadway show but subsequently joined the touring production.

"What role will you be playing?"

"Lorraine Sheldon."

"The provocative star actress. I know the play. Let's see if I can remember the characters."

He searched his memory and smiled fondly. It was a good play, although the last act dragged a bit, and he didn't care for the part in the play where the character Banjo traps Lorraine in an Egyptian sarcophagus, ready to be shipped off to Nova Scotia.

"Ah, yes, she's a glamorous and beautiful actress, isn't she? Sheridan Whiteside uses her to wreck his faithful secretary's marriage plans. What are her prime characteristics?" He tapped a finger against his chin, deep in thought. "She's temperamental, acid-tongued, and self-serving, isn't she? Bit of a gossip and a gold-digger, too. Hell, it's the perfect role for you. I reckon you'll have no trouble assimilating into that character."

"Very droll," she responded, unimpressed. "And to think, you were doing so well up until this point. How disappointing."

"Wait, I haven't finished. Isn't it true that a good actress can play any part and make it her own? I'm confident you could turn your acting chops to any of the roles and get a standing ovation," he added slyly.

"Nice recovery," she told him.

The waiter returned with their drinks, interrupting the conversation. As he put the glasses on the table, Ray was distracted by the color and texture of Merriam's beverage.

"It's the yummiest," she told him, purring at the sight of the thick, pink liquid in the stemmed cocktail glass.

"It looks like a milkshake," he remarked critically.

"It's a simple cocktail. The ingredients are three-quarter ounces of crème de noyaux, three-quarter ounces of white crème de cocoa, and one and a half ounces of heavy cream. Garnish with cherries and voilà!"

"Sounds disgusting," he declared.

"If you replace the heavy cream with a giant scoop of vanilla ice cream, it makes for the perfect dessert."

He laughed and reached for his glass. The Tom Collins tasted just right. A mix of gin, fresh lemon juice, syrup, and club soda, it was another refreshing but straightforward cocktail.

When he set the tall glass back down on the table next to hers, he remarked, "I do like the vibrant hue of yours. The color adds conversational value. By comparison, mine seems rather tame and unimpressive."

She nodded and said teasingly, "Don't you think a person's choice of drink says a great deal about them? On one side of the table, we have the staid and conventional Tom Collins; on the other, we have the fun, coquettish Pink Squirrel."

"You may be onto something. However, isn't the pink squirrel merely a combination of cream and sugar? After a few sips, the drinker grows sick of the saccharine taste and craves something mellow. Something subtler and more sophisticated."

She put her elbow on the table and tucked her hand under her chin. He examined her contemplatively, savoring her delectable, petite chin and the delicate curvature of her cheekbones.

"I would describe it as having a rich, substantive quality," she argued. "It tantalizes the taste buds and leaves you satiated."

Her provocative smile enamored him. "I'm coming around to

your way of thinking. The drink does, indeed, say something about the drinker. Fun, coquettish, complex. It certainly suits you."

He took another sip of his Tom Collins, wondering if it didn't taste just a tad less pleasurable than before.

"Perhaps you should order a different drink," she suggested. "Something that better reflects your personality."

"What do you advise?"

"How about the Manhattan's Scottish cousin, the Rob Roy?"

Ray searched his memory for the recipe. "Whiskey, vermouth, and a dash of aromatic bitters."

"This version has Scotch instead of rye whiskey and orange bitters instead of aromatic bitters."

"And how would you describe the result?"

"Interesting, if slightly odd, but in the long run, quite rewarding."

He signaled to the waiter, achieving quite the workout with his frantic hand movements, but, alas, he didn't have much success. Infuriatingly, Merriam could lure the man to their table without much effort.

An hour later, when Ray was nicely liquored up and cozy in his seat, he attempted to steer the conversation toward the pastor. Unhappily, he didn't get the opportunity. The waiter's appearance at their table was an unwelcome sight this time, and when the man passed a folded slip of note paper to Merriam, Ray watched with rising alarm.

"Is there a problem?" he asked, directing his question to either.

The waiter didn't pay him any notice, and Merriam didn't seem to hear him. She quickly unfolded the piece of paper and silently read the message. Eventually, she looked up at the waiter and said, "The bill, please."

The waiter gave a curt nod, inferring from her tone that she was keen to settle the bill posthaste.

"Anything the problem?" Ray asked Merriam as the waiter scurried away.

"I'm needed back at the church," she disclosed evenly.

"Work! At this time of night? Bit late for bookkeeping, isn't it? What's so urgent?" he asked, appalled.

"An accounting error," she explained. "I have to locate paperwork, that's all."

"Can't it wait until morning?"

"The pastor wouldn't send for me unless it's important," she said stubbornly.

"I don't see why it has to be this minute," continued Ray sulkily. He had been enjoying her company and had plans to extend their rendezvous until very late into the night.

"Sometimes, there are little fires to put out. They can happen at all times of the day. Luckily, I'm still in the neighborhood."

"Yes, isn't that lucky," he grumbled, watching her get to her feet.

The waiter had reappeared with the receipt in his hand.

Merriam politely rejected Ray's offer to pay. She took a money clip from her purse and handed it to the waiter, saying, "Please take what we owe and include a reasonable tip for yourself."

Having not seen the bill, it was difficult to gauge if the waiter took only a modest tip or something more rewarding. Either way, Merriam didn't care.

Ray got to his feet and insisted on accompanying Merriam to her workplace. "This isn't the right neighborhood for a girl to walk alone," he said.

"I'm capable of looking after myself," she complained.

"I don't doubt it. However, this isn't an offer; it's a demand. I won't let you go alone. My conscience won't let me."

She tried not to glare at him. He was determined to be a pest.

"Try to keep up," she conceded.

It was a balmy evening, almost pleasant if you took your time, but the walk was short and Merriam's pace brisk. When they reached the church entrance, she said goodbye to him. Her words were not tender or softly spoken. She made it clear that she wanted to get rid of him immediately, and he regarded her behavior as an unfair dismissal. It was as if she feared being seen with him.

Of course, it might also have been a case of her fearing what Ray might see—a peak beyond the parish doors, a glimpse of the other aspect of her life.

He waved and turned away, hiding his grimace. He was frustrated that their time had been cut short and annoyed that he hadn't established a further meeting.

As he walked away, wondering why she had been called back to work so late at night, it felt like a dozen eyes were watching him leave. There was a target on his back, he was sure of it, and his surveillance of Merriam had been terminated.

———— ✦ ————

On his return to the Hotel Buckminster, Ray stopped briefly at the reception desk to see if any messages had been left for him. This time, his nightly routine saw a payoff. When the receptionist handed him an envelope, he tore it open immediately. Despite the neat penmanship, his eyes stumbled over the words, but as he slowly reread the note, those russet brown eyes glinted with excitement.

The coded message from Walter highlighted irregular activities at the church earlier in the day. Dozens of boxed crates had lined the delivery bay, and a well-connected international antique and art dealer known as O'Reilly had made repeat appearances at the church.

Ray guessed that Sinclair was about to export a sizable hoard of his merchandise. He couldn't tell whether this marked the closure of his operation or its expansion.

Intriguingly, fierce confrontations between O'Reilly and Sinclair had then taken place. It was too early to know if their relationship had completely fallen apart, though clearly, a seismic quarrel percolated. To add to the intrigue, Sinclair had been spotted loading a suitcase into the trunk of his car.

Were these two incidents connected, Ray wondered? Walter believed they were. Ray's gut instincts told him that Sinclair was heavily invested in Boston, to the extent that he wouldn't willingly detach himself from his tight-knit community. The luggage in the trunk of his car hinted at a vacation rather than a plan to evacuate, and this was the piece of Walter's message that intrigued him the most. Where exactly did the reverend plan to go? And would he be traveling alone?

Ten

Without an informer closely attached to Sinclair's organization, it was an impossible task trying to track the reverend's day-to-day activities. Getting close to the man was even more challenging. He was like a clam, secretive and unknowable, continually concealed in a tightly closed shell, operating almost entirely within his house of prayer. In the evenings and mornings, he was escorted to and from his home by a man who looked like he could go ten rounds with Rocky Marciano. There was no regularity to the man's work schedule, no set time for him to begin or end his day.

The one constant was the alarming bustle of activity in and around the church in the daytime, with trucks, deliverymen, and churchgoers coming and going with orderliness. As Ray had discovered to his cost, watchful, hostile men patrolled the grounds, and a security guard policed the building at night. The church itself was a fortress, its smooth, high walls and security procedures something to scrutinize, admire, and want to emulate. It felt as if the only way inside was with a crack team of mercenaries.

Merriam had teased clues about the scope of their profitable work but offered no real answers about Sinclair and the extent of their relationship. That she was waitressing on the side hinted that she needed extra money, but the knowledge that Sinclair could summon her back to work late at night made Ray believe she was beholden to her job. Or beholden to the pastor.

Ray sat on the edge of his bed in his hotel room, looking at Walter's message again, reading it for the umpteenth time, exhilarated by thoughts of the suitcase, the colossal shipment, and the quarreling between Sinclair and O'Reilly. It was a message that brought hope and strength, offering the promise of impending change.

The unexpected bark of the telephone on his side table startled him, leading him to drop the notepaper. He sprang to his feet and snatched the receiver from the cradle, fumbling it but managing to secure it against his ear with his shoulder. The sound of Walter's voice didn't have a calming effect.

"Get over to Merriam's home," the old man urged. "Sinclair just left the church without his henchmen. We think he's headed to Merriam's place."

Ray glanced at his watch. "Hell, it's damn early," he muttered.

"We think he's leaving town. Something up, Ray. Can you catch up to Sinclair and find out what he's planning?"

"I'll get him," promised Ray.

He slammed the receiver down.

His belongings were well-ordered and systematically arranged in compartments in his luggage. He raced into the bathroom and gathered a few essential toiletries, shoving them into his bag, sabotaging the neat arrangement. Then he grabbed his jacket and hurried out of his hotel room.

Ray pulled on his jacket as he rode the elevator to the ground floor. He exited the building as if in a race, sprinting to his car. He was hampered only slightly by his bag. It wasn't clear whether he was checking out of the Hotel Buckminster or taking a day trip. Either way, he wanted to be prepared for all eventualities, and he believed that losing a few minutes to ensure he had some of his personal possessions was a wise move.

He opened the trunk of his car and hastily stowed his suitcase, panting heavily. The previous night's heavy drinking hadn't done him any favors, and he was of the opinion that the damn Rob Roy concoction Merriam had persuaded him to try ought to be outlawed.

He got in the driver's seat of his Buick and drove as fast as he could to Merriam's apartment building. Incredibly, as he cruised down her street, intending to find a convenient place to park, he was shocked to see Sinclair heading the opposite way in an Oldsmobile 88 sedan. As the car passed by him, Ray noticed Merriam in the passenger seat, fixated on the interior mirror, fastening a large barrette in her hair.

Ray steered his car into the nearest side road and made a nimble three-point turn. His car emerged onto the main street a couple of hundred meters behind Sinclair's sedan, and he managed to maintain that distance until they reached the highway. As he followed the Oldsmobile, trying not to weave in and out of traffic to keep up, he was conscious of the tremble in his hands. It wasn't alcohol withdrawal, at least not this time; his hands shook excitedly. He fought the urge to go hard on the accelerator, allowing the Oldsmobile to get almost out of sight.

In an effort to control his excitement, he reached over and fiddled with the car radio. He turned the dial until the WMEX station was tuned in, keen for rock-and-roll music. Then he lowered the driver's window, letting the morning air chill his face and the wind deconstruct his pompadour.

Barely half an hour into the journey, the Oldsmobile exited the highway and took a slow country road northwest. Ray eased off the gas some more, allowing Sinclair's car to stay far ahead. He was anticipating a long, scenic drive, but it turned out to be neither of those things.

After a few miles, he reached a small farming town with a population of just over sixteen thousand. He turned off his radio and slowed his car to twenty miles per hour as he approached the town center. He saw no sign of the Oldsmobile as he surveyed the streets. He increased speed and passed through the town, continuing on the main road.

Less than two minutes later, he was relieved to spot the back end of Sinclair's car. Not wanting to draw attention to himself, he reduced his speed again, following the sedan for a few more minutes, keeping at a cautious distance.

Sinclair's sedan eventually came to a halt outside a no-frills diner with the ominous name Dirty Fork. Ray took his time parking his car and remained in his seat long enough to allow Sinclair and Merriam to get settled at a table in the eatery.

He opened the trunk of his car and foraged around in his suitcase, extracting the black wig and the horn-rimmed spectacles. He worried that the hair was too long, too feminine and that it looked too theatrical. Did it draw attention to his face rather than conceal his true appearance, he wondered? Was it obvious he was wearing a toupee? Did the wig mar the effect of the glasses?

A careful examination in the interior mirror assured him that the hairpiece was fine and that the glasses added character. In point of fact, the spectacles did wonders to improve his confidence, convincing him he looked like a different person—a Clark Kent version of Superman. But would Merriam see through the disguise?

He was competent at masking his voice and managing to be inconspicuous, and he accepted the dangers of being recognized. Even if he didn't learn anything useful from the minister's lips, a mug of coffee and a lightly toasted bagel with a thick spread of cream cheese was never an exercise in futility.

Ray waited for five minutes and then grabbed his packet of business papers off the passenger seat, got out of the car, and strolled confidently into the diner. He surveyed the room, his eyes quickly assessing the faces of the various patrons. Though it was far busier than Ray had anticipated, the animated voices around him put him at ease. Nobody paid him great attention and the notion that he looked like a performer about to take to the stage for a theater production instantly dissolved. Plenty of tables and booths were unoccupied, adding to his relief.

He spotted Sinclair and Merriam and made his way toward them, moving through the room at speed. Whatever reservations he had previously held about Merriam recognizing him were immediately allayed when he sat at the table nearest her. She looked straight at him, their eyes locking for an instant, and unless she was well-versed in the art of deception, there was no indication that she recalled ever having seen him before.

The biggest test for Ray was when the waitress came over to take his order. He began by asking for coffee, but the sounds that came out of his mouth were not dissimilar to the harsh, scraping noise the leg of a wooden chair makes when dragged across ceramic tiles. To his horror, he noticed Sinclair cast a disdainful look in his direction.

Ray softened his accent and ordered a bagel with cream cheese. Thankfully, the reverend didn't take offense at the gentler pitch of Ray's voice. Ray then opened the bulky paper file in front of him and arranged the bundle of papers across the tabletop. It was an effort sifting through it all, and after a short while, he yearned to toss the stack of papers under his table. Walter had gone to great lengths to build an identity for Ray but neglected to fully define his work. Exactly what was sold and to whom was a mystery.

"Who the hell cares?" had been Walter's response to Ray's inquiry.

As Ray waited for his coffee, he thumbed through the sales slips until it became a chore. The sight of the waitress returning to his table carrying a coffee pot marked a happy respite.

While she poured the coffee, Ray glanced over her shoulder at Sinclair, trying to gauge the man's mood. The blank expression told him nothing.

Ray drizzled sugar into his cup and gently stirred the liquid, casting furtive glances at the reverend, wishing the man would signpost his feelings. Sinclair's holy status intrigued him. Temptation and opportunity lured most men to acts of sin, but here was a man who profited from the façade of saintliness. He had built an empire of racketeers and thieves within the consecrated walls of his egregious house of prayer. The deity this man worshipped was Plutus, the Greek god of wealth, riches, and abundance.

When his bagel arrived, Ray feigned interest in it, but he couldn't take his eyes off Sinclair. He was fascinated by the odious man and the strange dynamic between him and the beautiful Merriam. The silver-haired reverend, boyishly handsome, had a soft but rhythmic quality to his voice. Eloquent and persuasive, his silver tongue captivated Merriam. She had a perpetual smile on her face and was unable to take her eyes off the reverend whenever his lips moved. Demon worship was at play here. Ray was sure of it.

As for Sinclair, he habitually pawed at Merriam's slender but shapely thigh, the determined glint in his flinty gray eyes revealing he could scarcely restrain his passions. The food was pushed from one side of his plate to the other without purpose. His hunger was purely for the woman sitting beside him.

Ray dipped his knife into the pot of cream cheese, sullenly gouging cuts in the soft mixture, his eyes fixed on Merriam, appreciating the delicate contours of her face. He disapproved of the way she stared at Sinclair, wishing there wasn't such fondness in her smile. Then his eyes drifted to her splendid, cream-colored blouse, which was indecently tight but showed off her chest magnificently, and he found himself salivating. She had the face of a goddess, her body the shape of a centerfold. He watched her adoringly, oblivious to how his knife stabbed the cream cheese, tearing into the gooey mixture with crazed menace.

Ray was suddenly conscious that he was making a scene. He placed the knife on his plate and reached for his coffee. He took a long, measured sip, his eyes returning to Merriam. He watched her appetizing lips and studied them as she talked. Her voice was quiet, the words muffled, but he could read those delectable lips and decipher much of what was spoken to Sinclair.

"Must you leave tonight?"

Sinclair's inaudible response frustrated Ray, yet some words were distinguishable: "…must… O'Reilly…trouble."

Sinclair dropped his voice a shade lower, the soft hum of his tone only clear to the woman beside him. Despite Sinclair's attempts to veil their discussion, Ray's unblinking eyes watched the man's lips intently, gathering a basic level of comprehension from the enunciated words. "O'Reilly," "tonight," and "Hanson" were the pointers Ray picked up on.

Merriam's inquiring eyes and the words "Hanson" and "custodian" helped Ray assemble the clues. As they continued to talk, Ray imagined the extent of their conversation:

"Can't it wait until tomorrow?"

A shake of the head. "Better to deal with O'Reilly tonight when there's no one else around. I told Hanson I'd talk with that conniving rat myself. I don't plan on being long, my darling. Just a thirty-minute drive each way, then an hour at the church at most. I'll be back here no later than ten o'clock."

"Can't you talk to O'Reilly over the telephone?"

"If only it was that simple. He's intent on seeing the merchandise before we transport it. He has it in his head that we plan to double-cross him. I don't know what put that idea into his head. Naturally suspicious, I guess. Probably because it's the sort of thing he might do."

"What are you going to do when you see him?"

"Let him examine the crates, of course."

"Is that wise? What if he's planning something?"

"He wouldn't dare. Besides, I can look after myself."

Ray hoped he hadn't let his imagination run amok. Sinclair's thoughts seemed clear, his words full of sense and reason, but Ray couldn't shake the feeling that he had read more into the couple's conversation than was sensible. What if it was all pure conjecture?

He was staking his life on the conviction that he could read lips and competently divine what was left unspoken.

"Let's get out of here," he distinctly heard Merriam say.

Sinclair wiped his mouth with a napkin and signaled to the waitress, waving the serviette about like it was a little white flag of surrender. The waitress acknowledged him, and as she moved to return the carafe to the warming plate, Ray interrupted her journey, politely asking for more coffee. While she refilled his cup, he asked for the check. She nodded, insisting she would be back in a moment, but then instantly walked to Sinclair's table and started talking to him.

Ray guzzled his coffee, emptying the cup in one swift motion. The coffee was hot but not scalding, and he somehow managed to empty the cup without a problem. He watched the reverend and the waitress, surprised about the length of their conversation. The man was prattling on endlessly, perhaps practicing his next sermon. Ray chewed on his bagel while he waited for the check. He was focused on the waitress, unable to concentrate on anything else. The thought of Sinclair and Merriam departing the diner first made him panicky.

Sinclair got to his feet, puffing like it was an effort. He hadn't pigged out on his meal and didn't act like he was bloated and in need of a wheelchair to escort him out of the joint, and yet he rubbed his stomach and grimaced as if he felt a bout of diarrhea coming on. Merriam elbowed him, pressing him to get a move on, and he delved into his pocket and threw some bank notes onto the table with frustration. The look he gave the money intimated that it was a tip given begrudgingly. In fact, there was a moment when he looked like he was contemplating putting some of it back in his pocket.

Merriam gave Sinclair another elbow, and he nodded, put his arm around her, and gave her a good squeeze. Then he escorted her out of the diner, pulling her close, struggling to walk straight.

Ray put the last piece of his bagel into his mouth, chewing it frantically. The prospect of losing track of the reverend unnerved him. Unfortunately, his chunk of bagel had hardened, and he struggled to grind it down. His coffee cup was now empty, and the bagel seemed to be lodged in his throat.

He put his hand in the air and waggled it about for a bit, and people stared at him like he was mad; the waitress didn't notice a thing. His wave became an extravagant, frenzied gesture, and then the hand turned into a fist, and Ray started waving that about, growling loudly, pretending he was clearing his throat. He almost choked on his partially masticated wedge of bagel.

The waitress was busy at the cash register and writing up the receipts. Her penmanship was exceptional, and she was a marvel at the money side of things.

Ray craned his neck to see past the old couple in a booth by the window and caught sight of the reverend getting into his Oldsmobile. He shouted boorishly to the waitress, "That check ready yet?"

The impatience in his voice antagonized her. She scowled at him but uttered no complaint.

Ray stared out the window and groaned as the Oldsmobile reversed out of the parking lot and turned onto the main road. In frustration, he got to his feet, unwilling to wait a second longer.

The waitress met him as he was halfway to the door. "Here," he said, thrusting bills into her hand. "Keep the change."

He scurried out of the diner and jogged to his car. When his vehicle pulled out of the parking lot, he wasn't sure if he could catch up to the Oldsmobile. Though convinced that Sinclair was headed to Boston, he didn't want to jump to any conclusions. He hit the gas and sped down the street, thundering through the peaceful countryside.

A mile later, he caught sight of Sinclair's sedan. He followed the car for several miles, keeping his distance. Eventually, it pulled into a parking lot with a large neon sign out front that read: New England Motor Court. The lights in some of the letters had long since burned out.

Ray trundled past the motor court and saw the Oldsmobile stop in the parking space outside the main office. Discovering Sinclair and Merriam returning to their favorite squalid rendezvous location was like a dream come true. He had imagined this moment vividly for the past five weeks but never actually expected to witness it happen.

Ray stepped on the gas and continued down the road a little farther, deciding to circle the block a few times and familiarize himself with the area. Although he wanted to allow Sinclair sufficient time to secure accommodation, he needed to know which cabin they had secured.

His eyes explored the neighborhood with curiosity. It was a depressed area with a full quota of boarded-up homes and closed businesses. Ugly graffiti adorned the walls of buildings, making Ray wonder what had enticed Sinclair to stay in such a mediocre town in the first place. It wasn't quite scenic, it wasn't quite rural, and it wasn't private or secluded. In fact, nothing seemed all that appealing. As the reverend wasn't short of cash, it didn't make much sense. Bringing one's mistress to a place such as this might be construed as disrespectful, and Ray took umbrage at the fact that he, too, would have to book a night there.

When he pulled into the parking lot, he was surprised to see Sinclair and Merriam walking out of the main office. Ray headed for the far end of the lot and pulled in between an old station wagon and a dented Packard Club Coupe. He cut the engine and waited, staring at Merriam through the back window. She picked lint off her blouse and smoothed down her hair. Sinclair rummaged around in the trunk of his car, taking his time. He put his modest overnight bag on the ground, reached back into the trunk, and hauled out an oversized suitcase. The pink ribbon wrapped around the handle told Ray it was Merriam's luggage.

Sinclair closed the trunk lid. As he straightened, he moved his hands to the lower part of his back, wincing a little. His frame was broad, and the narrow cut of his button-down shirt revealed his rotund stomach. He stared at Merriam as she ambled toward their cabin, and his body seemed to sigh. With gritted teeth, he picked up both pieces of luggage and lumbered after her.

Ray lingered in his car until they had entered their cabin. Before he went to the main office, he sauntered past the row of spacious units, making a mental note of Sinclair's door number.

Removed from his formidable posse of thugs, the usually careful reverend had allowed himself to become isolated and vulnerable. The situation was almost too good to be true, making Ray wary about Sinclair's motives. It didn't make sense why a careful, well-protected man would suddenly drop his guard and hole up in this ghost town. Although Ray was aware that the couple had made prior visits to this motel, he felt that something was amiss. A vital piece of information had escaped him, an obvious answer as to why the reverend was traveling without a security detail.

As Ray wandered over to the main office, he eyeballed the beat-up vehicles in the parking lot and realized his gleaming new car stood out like a blazing fire in the dead of night. It might have been more sensible to rent a humble car in Boston than show off his expensive Roadmaster Riviera.

He shrugged it off. It was poor judgment, but he felt confident he would get away with the mistake. Then he stepped into the office.

Eleven

The surly, barrel-chested man behind the reception desk glowered at Ray. He was that way with a lot of the guests, but in this case, he simply didn't like the cut of Ray's jib.

Ray noticed the big gold nametag pinned to the man's patterned shirt, which displayed the word manager in bold letters. Unmoved by the man's hostile glare, he said, "I need a room for the night. When I pulled in here, I didn't see a sign out front with the nightly rate."

He stressed the word *nightly*, presuming from the slightly squalid state of the main office that there was also an hourly rate. The establishment rivaled the Slate Gray Motor Hotel in terms of dinginess and austerity.

The manager muttered incomprehensively and opened the guestbook. The noise of the spine of the book smacking against his desk muffled his remark.

Ray sighed as he reached into his pocket and pulled out a thick wad of cash. The idea of spending a night in this place and paying for the pleasure was a little galling. He removed the money clip and unfolded the bank notes, making sure that the manager got a nice long look at his bundle of money. There were a lot of fins and sawbucks and plenty of Jacksons. There were even some deuces in there somewhere. It was largely padded with singles, with the larger denominations at the top of the bankroll for effect.

The manager was rough-looking, with two days' growth on

his chin and piggish eyes. The piggish eyes widened at the sight of the dough, and he automatically started computing the amount in Ray's hand, licking his lips as he silently counted. He was the type of man who didn't keep much change in his pockets. Mostly, he spent his earnings before it had a chance to get comfortable in his wallet.

"That's a lot of cash you're carrying, pal," he muttered, unable to take his eyes off the greenbacks.

"Uh-huh. I like to come prepared."

"You rob a bank or something?"

"Think I'd tell you if I did?"

"Guess not," conceded the manager. "*Did* you, though?"

"No, nothing like that," Ray smirked. The robbery would come later. "I just haven't had a chance to deposit this week's pay. Now, about that room. You got a vacant cabin or not?"

"Just how long are you planning on staying?"

"One night. Planning to get up early tomorrow and pull out of here as soon as it's light."

The manager grunted indifferently. His gaze returned to the bankroll. "It'll be six bucks."

Ray peeled six singles from the bottom of his stack and slid the money across the counter. "I'll take cabin eight."

The manager rested his hand over the top of the money. "Cabin eight is a double. You can have five. That's a single."

"I prefer left-facing rooms," Ray explained. "I'll stick with eight."

The man's eyes narrowed with suspicion. "You got company?"

"No. I'm alone."

"Then you had better take a different cabin, mister. A double is twelve bucks."

"Twelve? That all? That's fine with me."

The manager stared at him intensely, like a mind-reader trying to unravel his secrets. He didn't look pleased by what he saw, either. He didn't want any trouble, and the deceit in those russet brown eyes persuaded him that this traveler was nothing but trouble.

"Stick with the single room," he insisted.

"Can't do that," said Ray with a stern shake of his head. "Eight's the one I got my eye on."

"You been here before?"

Ray shook his head.

"Listen, mister, I had my share of problems yesterday. A persnickety fella from Wisconsin smashed a dresser. Said he was trying to rearrange the furniture in his cabin to his liking. Wanted to wriggle out of paying for the damage, too."

In point of fact, the man had damaged furniture while trying to kill vermin. His complaints about bedbugs and cockroaches hadn't impressed the manager, so he threatened to file a report to the local health department about the horrors of a night at the New England Motor Court. He was also keen to get the local newspapers interested and see if he couldn't get the place rebranded as New England's leading site to find the biggest and best cockroach colonies. Somehow, the situation had been resolved amicably, but not until the manager had fetched his shotgun.

"What's that gotta do with me?" asked Ray.

"Accommodating the whims of finicky guests is one thing, but I got a feeling there's a damn good reason you want that particular cabin. Has nothing to do with feng shui, neither."

"This ain't The Plaza Hotel," said Ray crossly. "I don't see a line of Cadillacs outside, and I don't imagine you're booked up with reservations all month. There some reason you want to turn away money?"

The man watched him distrustfully. "Why are you so set on a double, huh? You got a broad coming later?"

"I should be so lucky."

"I don't want any trouble here, mister. This is a respectable joint."

Ray sneered. "Of course it is. I'm sure the police wouldn't dream of raiding this place."

"That's right," said the manager, tetchily. "You insinuating there's something disreputable about the place?" He was contemplating getting a hold of the shotgun under his desk.

Ray shook his head, although the telling pause before he did so didn't please the office manager.

"We offer great in-room features and entertainment. Air-cooling systems in each cabin, as well as a television set. And just like The Plaza Hotel, we even have a direct-dial telephone system. You won't find a more desirable, upscale motor court in all of New England, and I want to keep it that way."

Ray waved away his concerns. "Look, the company I work for is covering my expenses while I'm traveling through the East Coast, drumming up sales," he explained. "I thought I'd treat myself to a nice place for a change before I start out on the long drive back. Something more spacious. I'm not looking for trouble. I've no ulterior motive." He peeled off a ten-dollar bill and slapped it on the counter. "Here, this should cover the cost. And keep the change."

The man looked at the ten-dollar note like it was dirty money.

"I didn't mean to get your horns up." Ray returned the rest of his money to his pocket. "Write me up a receipt, will you."

The manager's eyes bore into Ray, trying to gauge his honesty. Finally, he closed his hand around the banknotes and stashed them in his cash register. Then he went and got the key to cabin number eight and placed it on the desk.

"Much obliged," said Ray, trying not to let his relief show.

"Just don't rearrange the furniture," the manager advised. "Break anything, and you pay for the damages. Got it?"

"Sure. I'm no interior decorator, so I'm not itching to give the rooms a makeover if that's what you think. But I'll be mindful and watch I don't put a hole through the door or kick over the ottoman."

He picked up the key and went straight to his cabin. A quick survey of his rooms warned him to be extra gentle with the rickety furniture. The doors to the closet were loose and about ready to come off at the hinges with a solid yank. The manager appeared to run a crafty side business in screwing over the guests. A broken door here, a collapsed sofa there…all he needed were a few heavy-handed patrons each week, and he would have a steady stream of extra income passing through his grasping hands.

Ray then went straight to the writing desk in the living room and used the telephone to call Walter. The man answered the call surprisingly quickly—his Swedish masseuse must have finished with him early. Ray began to fill him in on what had happened during the day, but Walter cut him off abruptly.

"Thank God you telephoned, Ray. I've been trying to get a message to you. Where are you?"

"The New England Motor Court."

"Is the reverend there?"

"Yes, he just checked in with his doxy."

"Merriam?"

"Yes, Merriam. Who else? I have the cabin next to them."

"Listen, Ray. There have been some new developments. The worst kind."

Ray's stomach muscles tightened as he heard the swelling panic in Walter's voice. "Okay, you got my attention. My heart is kicking like a drowning kitten, for Christ's sake. What's the story?"

"Carter's been spotted in Boston with his goons. Seems that somebody tipped him off about the reverend. He's come for Hessman's Necklace."

Ray gave an involuntary shudder. His nerves didn't often get the better of him, but right now, he could feel scorching pricks of anxiety surging up and down his back. "How long do you reckon I've got?"

"Can't say for sure, but I'm guessing it isn't long. A day or two, if we're lucky. He's not a patient man. Acts on impulse."

"Yes, I've heard the stories. Nickname is Blazing Gun. Shoots first and asks questions later."

"Not quite," Walter corrected. "Blazing Rage is the nickname. And it's not just a gun he uses. You remember the Greek thieves?"

"The Notaras gang."

"He tortured them to death, one by one, with each man helplessly watching while he butchered their compadres. Scalped his victims, much like the Apache and Sioux Indians. It's said that he keeps the scalps in glass cabinets in his ghoulish private museum. They're not small disks of skin, either, but the whole haired scalp, including the ears."

Ray could taste bile in his mouth. He suddenly longed for a good long slug of whiskey. "Do we know where Carter is now?"

"Not exactly. I can hazard a guess at his plans, though. He'll have positioned his men around the church to monitor security, and very soon, they're going to conclude that the best way is to capture Sinclair and go through the front door with automatic guns and a knife pressed to the reverend's throat. They'll need him alive, of course, if they want to get inside his safe. The rest of the poor sods will end up as corpses."

Ray scratched his chin pensively. "Can you assemble a team to stop him?"

"The surveillance crew I have in place knows to call me the moment anything happens. I won't put them in harm's way, but we have resources we can call on if absolutely necessary."

"What about the motor court? You think Sinclair was tailed here?"

"Very likely," admitted Walter.

Instinctively, Ray's hand moved to the shoulder holster beneath his jacket. His eyes drifted to the window by the door, and his fingers strayed to the .357 Magnum in his holster. Anyone tailing Sinclair would have quickly realized that Ray was tailing him also, and naturally, Ray's involvement implicated Walter. Hell, it was rapidly becoming a high-stakes chess match with all the key pieces exposed.

"Is the necklace even real?" Ray asked.

"It's real."

"All you have is that photograph. What if it's a fake?"

"It's real."

"Somebody cooked up this wild tale to pit you and Carter against one another."

"No," said Walter, adamantly.

"And I'm the sap in the line of fire, about to get wiped out," continued Ray. "All because of a make-believe treasure."

"That photograph is no fake," insisted Walter, irked by the notion. "It's been analyzed carefully. It's authentic, I promise you."

"Let's assume it's real, and let's assume that the reverend is damn fool enough to bring it with him to this flee-pit so his mistress can model it for him in bed. If his cabin is being monitored, that doesn't give me many options. I've got to steal into the room in the dead of night and pry it off her neck while she's sleeping. Then I've got to get out of there in one piece without my shadow putting a bullet in my back."

"Attaboy," said Walter, encouragingly. "That about sums it up. You've been in tighter spots, Ray, and you always pull through."

"I don't care for the setup this time," said Ray dismally.

"You're being paid well for a reason. What did you think it was going to be like? A walk in the park? Nothing is easy, but nothing is impossible, either. Find a way, and get it done fast," Walter said sternly. "Now, give me your telephone number. I'll call you if I hear any news."

---- ◆ ----

Ray kept to his room, trying to rest his body but unable to stay still. After moving from the bed to the chair and back again, he hovered by the window, slouched against the wall. Cars would occasionally come and go, but the motor court wasn't humming with life, and the hours slid by without incident, the sounds from the cabin next door negligible. Ray began to pace up and down his room, unhappy that he couldn't see into the neighboring cottages, fretting about Carter and O'Reilly and Sinclair's imminent big shipment. The lack of useful data was driving him crazy.

The uneventful hours wore him down. Sinclair and Merriam hadn't left their cabin in hours. They hadn't eaten since breakfast. Ray hadn't either. He was hungry and confused, continually distracted, and by the early evening, he could scarcely take it anymore. He exited his cottage and walked to his car to gather his belongings. The sun was setting, but the temperature was still hot. He took his time, relishing the humidity and enjoying the last moments of sunlight. When he returned to the cabin, he felt a little more patient and untroubled, more like his old self.

He set his luggage on the floor and his briefcase on the bed. Now was the time for some serious thinking, he concluded, unclasping the latches and opening the case. The bottle of whiskey practically rolled into his hand. He grabbed it by the neck and fetched a glass from the kitchenette, pouring himself a generous measure. He glugged it like water, enjoying the warm sensation in his throat. He planned to pour himself another and take his time with it, but a tiny glint of light across the windowpane distracted him. He put down the glass and went to the window, staring at the gleaming Ford Courier that pulled up. He remained at the window, clutching the curtain, watching a young couple exit the vehicle. There was a bottle of wine in the woman's hand, and although it was nearly impossible to deduce the color of the liquid or read the label on the glass, Ray determined from the woman's youthful face and the way she carelessly allowed the contents to swish around that it was a low-priced beginner's red, probably a pinot noir or a merlot.

He continued gazing out of the window long after the couple entered their cottage. It had been a lazy and soothing afternoon with clear blue skies and no wind. It was the type of day where it would have been nice to take a long stroll and exercise his lungs, not stay cooped up indoors.

The sky was becoming bluer, nightfall imposing itself, and the passion of the summer sun beginning to wane. Though peaceful and pleasant, he knew this was a time for inactivity, a chance to mentally prepare for the inevitable showdown. Divine intervention had brought him to this significant venue with Sinclair and Merriam within meters of him, close enough to snoop on and plot a housebreak. Ray sat and thought about the shape of their suitcases, fantasizing about what might be cushioned between the garments or secured in the side pockets. Did she have pearls with her? A Tiffany Soleste platinum ring with a ruby and diamonds? Was that a Rolex watch he had seen on Sinclair's wrist earlier? How much loot did the treasure-seeking Holy Joe keep in the lockbox?

Ray felt certain the necklace was among the reverend's belongings, just as he was sure it would be in his possession by the end of his stay.

He pulled a packet of Lucky Strike cigarettes from his pocket and tore off the flavor-protective foil, craving the Middle Eastern tartness and the mellow, fragrant aftertaste. His thoughts were clearer when he was swathed in a dense, pungent swirl of tobacco smoke. Placing a cigarette lightly between his lips, he dug around in his pockets for a matchbook. He didn't find one, however, and had to rest the unlit cigarette on the edge of the ashtray while he moved the search to his car. Eventually, he located a matchbook in the glove compartment.

The branches of the lofty trees at the back of the cottages waved to him as he returned to his front door, bidding him goodnight. The soft breeze on his neck was a welcome sensation, although he was surprised by the slight change in the weather.

When he stepped back into his cabin, the telephone was ringing. He cast a wistful glance at the cigarette as he picked up the receiver.

"I've been trying to get through to you for the past ten minutes, Ray," griped Walter. "There have been new developments. Carter and his men have hit the church."

"You mean there's been a shootout?"

"Not quite. Carter and four others converged on the church, approaching it from all sides, armed with guns and knives. The security guard didn't put up much of a fight."

"Was he in on it?"

"I wouldn't think so. They knifed him in the throat. He died very quickly," said Walter, matter-of-factly. "His body was dragged away, put in the back of a truck. Carter's men used a battering ram to smash their way through the church door."

"Are they inside?"

"Yes. My surveillance man believes he heard a gunshot."

"Do we know if anyone called the police?"

"There's some activity on the streets. Trucks have been pulling up in the back lot, but there are no signs of a skirmish, and nothing else has been heard from inside. By the looks of those trucks, something is about to happen."

"Any markings on the trucks? Any indication of who sent them? Could they be Sinclair's suppliers?"

"Possibly, but they could also be Carter's. They haven't moved for five minutes. Seems like they're waiting for a signal."

"A signal to do what? Reinforcements?" Ray asked absently, working his thumb into the dimple on his chin.

"A signal to open their doors and prepare for loading. Judging by the size of the trucks, Sinclair must have a lot of merchandise in the safe room."

"If Sinclair's as well connected as you say, and that church is as well stocked with ancient treasures as we think, Carter's haul will be incredible. It's a better score than most bank jobs."

"It most certainly is," said Walter, sounding bitter. "Where's Sinclair? Does he know what's going on?"

"He's here at the motor court. He hasn't left his room since this morning."

A noise outside caught Ray's attention. It sounded like

someone had been heavy-handed with the door of their cottage.

"Hold on," he said, setting the receiver down.

He walked over to the window and gently adjusted the curtain. Sinclair had finally left his cabin and was strolling briskly across the parking lot. Ray watched him closely, trying to gauge the man's body language. The fading light and the grimy windowpane made it difficult to make out the expression on Sinclair's face. Nothing in his stride convinced Ray that he was aware of the burglary. Or else he was hiding his panic well.

Sinclair got into his Oldsmobile and eased the door shut. The engine growled to life a moment later, and the headlights flicked on. As he reversed, the twin beams flared in Ray's face.

Ray drew back from the window, needlessly concerned about being seen. The thud of the door in the cabin next door drew him back to the window. He squinted through the glass and saw Merriam scampering across the parking lot.

Gone were her skirt and blouse and the kitten-heel shoes, and now all she had on was a sheer lace nightie and a pair of house slippers. The headlights briefly revealed the translucent quality of the material as she ran across the front of the car to the driver's door. The reverend stopped abruptly, put the car in park, and opened his door.

Ray could tell by the desperate way Merriam grabbed the reverend that she was in a manic state. She hauled him out of his seat by his tie and held him tightly, determined not to let him leave. Sinclair, angered by her actions, fought to extricate himself.

While Ray scrutinized Merriam, deciphering her agitated behavior, his eyes came to rest on the heavy, sparkling jewelry clasped around her neck.

"My God," he muttered. "The necklace!"

A shiver of excitement went through him at the sight of the exquisite, emerald-studded adornment. He gazed at her in perplexed wonder, shocked at her conduct. She was practically sending Ray a covert invitation to burglarize her beautiful body.

As the reverend shook her roughly, chastising her for displaying her priceless jewelry in public, Merriam put a hand over her necklace, unaware that the damage had already been done. Slightly at odds with his savage manner, Sinclair leaned forward and planted his lips on hers. Rough yet full of passion, it had a calming effect on the woman, whose body went limp in his arms. The reverend held her firmly for a moment, then squeezed her shoulder affectionately and eased her away from him. She stepped back and watched dolefully as Sinclair got back into the vehicle and closed the door. While he reversed the car onto the main road, she hurried back across the parking lot to her cabin.

The faint noises from the telephone receiver sent Ray scampering across the room. "Walter, you still there?" he said into the handset.

"What the hell's going on?" Walter grumbled.

"I've just seen Sinclair leave. He's on his way back to the church. Merriam just kissed him goodbye in her negligee."

"No wonder you were gone so long," grouched Walter. "You've been gawping at her this whole time."

"Guess what else she was wearing?"

"Stockings and suspenders?"

Ray chuckled. "She was wearing the most delightful necklace you ever saw."

"Hessman's Necklace?" asked Walter, breathlessly.

"The genuine artifact, as far as I can tell. Or a beautiful imitation."

"Well, goddamn!" muttered Walter, relishing the prospect of finally getting his hands on the piece. "Where is the reverend's girl now?"

"She's returned to her cabin?"

"Then go get her."

"With pleasure."

He returned the receiver to its cradle and cracked his knuckles. Then he fetched the shoulder holster from the briefcase and strapped it on, adjusting the straps until it fitted snugly. After another quick examination of the Magnum, he slid it into his holster and got into his jacket.

Seeing the switchblade on the dresser, he seized it and shoved it in his pocket. Then he got the lock pick set, selected an appropriate pick and a tension wrench, and headed for the door.

Twelve

The fear of Sinclair returning made Ray move nimbly toward Merriam's cottage, keen not to squander minutes. The parking lot was quiet, and the onset of night comforted him. He gently inserted the pick and tension wrench into the keyway with confidence and went to work. His familiarity with locks and his years of experience as a professional burglar enabled him to force the door in less than two minutes. Then he put his tools in his pocket and opened the door.

As it moved inward, he remained motionless in the doorway, expecting to hear Merriam scream. The uncomfortable stillness in the cabin brought goosebumps to his flesh, and he reached inside his jacket, pulling the .357 Magnum from his shoulder holster. Although he didn't intend to use the gun, he hoped the sight of it might dissuade Merriam from doing something rash.

His eyes danced across the living quarters, observing nothing but the typical assortment of shabby furniture. There was a teak, drop-leaf dining table with a wobbly leg and a paddle armchair with ginger velvet upholstery that looked great from a distance but might fall apart if you put too much weight on it. Similar junkyard furnishings crowded his own cabin, elevating the look of the bleak space but adding no real value.

Ray carefully eased the cabin door closed, treading lightly. The only sound was the faint noise of the soles of his shoes padding across the Saxony smooth carpeting.

His eyes explored the room, delving into the shadows, surprised that Merriam was nowhere to be found. Though marginally larger than the cottage next door, the layout was a mirror image of his own, and the illustrated wallflower wallpaper with its darkly blue background was just as revolting. His gaze then stopped on the bathroom door, and the fact that it was closed hinted she was inside. Automatically, he twisted the doorknob and gave the door a gentle shove. The creaking sound as it moved inward made him adjust his grip on the firearm, ready to strike Merriam with the butt of the weapon if she attacked him.

The absence of sound within alarmed him, and he began to doubt if Merriam had really returned to the cabin. His mind went back to the sound he had heard earlier. Had she entered the cabin and shut the door or merely pulled the cabin door shut and gone elsewhere? Was it possible she was still outside, he wondered?

He cast a quick glance around the bathroom. His gun was angled into the empty bathtub as he peered beyond the shower curtain.

When he exited the room, the notion that she might be hiding in the living room made him pause in the doorway. He hadn't paid the main room much attention and began to wonder if she was in the bed, beneath the covers, or crouched beside the sectional couch. Those minutes spent picking the lock might have alerted her to his presence, and she would have had plenty of time to find a suitable hiding spot, he concluded.

As he peered around the room, he heard the eerie creaking noise of the bathroom door. The light, chilling sound made the hairs stand on his neck. An instant later, the door hit him hard in the shoulder, sending him stumbling forward. His fumbling fingers played with the gun like some novice juggler, and then a wooden clothes hanger whacked him painfully on the side of his head, the assault accompanied by a woman's malicious growl.

He fell, dropping to one knee, and the hunk of wood struck him again, rapping him on the knuckles. The gun jumped out of his hand and dropped to the floor, and as he reached for it, the piece of wood clipped him on the shoulder, preventing him from getting to it. He fell sideways, slumped across the floor, looking up at his attacker. He saw the broken clothes hanger in Merriam's hand and the aggression in her eyes. The hostility toward him was ghastly.

She suddenly turned and ran toward the door, and the sign of fear enticed him back to his feet. He covered the distance between them in two long strides and leaped on her back, slamming his hands on her shoulder blades. She crumpled under his weight, and they fell, landing inches from the door.

He pinned her beneath him, putting weight on her back, trapping her so thoroughly that she couldn't move. The pressure on her back was insufferable, and she could scarcely breathe. She was sure that he was about to crush her ribs or break her back. She tried to tell him, but his left hand closed around her mouth, smothering her screams and jailing her complaints.

The two of them remained on the floor in that position for nearly a quarter of an hour, and then he slackened his grip, convinced that he had effectively subdued her wrath.

When he removed his fingers from her face, she murmured weakly, "Get off me. Please."

He shifted his knees, releasing some pressure on her back, and he heard the relief in her voice as she moaned. Evidently in pain, she began to sob quietly, unable to move.

"I'll let you up if you behave yourself," he told her. "Promise me you'll be good."

"I will. I'll be good," Merriam said wearily between sobs.

He noticed drops of blood on his hand and realized she had accidentally bit her tongue during their struggle. He was so angry and humiliated by the surprise attack that he felt no sympathy for her.

"Do this right, and we can avoid any nasty business," he assured her.

He wanted to believe there would be no more trouble, but her earlier conduct persuaded him otherwise. The fight hadn't gone out of her, not yet. He was sure of that.

He climbed off her and attempted to help her to her feet. Instantly, she lashed out at him, raking her nails across his cheek with cruel intent.

He yelled in pain, and without a second thought, he grabbed her by the throat, maneuvering his body behind her so he was in the rear naked choke position. She grabbed his arms, ineffectively trying to get out of the chokehold. It took about nine unpleasant seconds before his grappling hold rendered her unconscious.

Ray immediately eased his grip on her throat and gathered her in his arms. He carried her into the living room, setting her down on the bed. Walter's earlier remark about stockings and suspenders spurred him to explore Merriam's small suitcase in the luggage rack by the bed.

Having emptied the contents over the floor, he rummaged through the pile of clothes, finding a pair of thick nylon stockings, which he used to restrain her wrists, and a silk scarf long enough to bind her ankles. Satisfied with his handiwork, he lifted her off the bed, moving her to a yellow chrome diner side chair. She flopped in the seat, unconscious, and he had to wrestle her into a better position so she didn't slide out.

He agitatedly glanced at his beautiful Omega Seamaster wristwatch with the jet-black dial, gold hands, and markers. It was a civilian version of the watch supplied to RAF pilots during World War II. This one had the advantage of automatic winding. Seeing the hands display nine o'clock produced a prickly sensation under his shirt collar. He took a deep breath and tried to quell his escalating panic. The way he had squandered the last twenty minutes was unforgivable.

He walked across the room and picked up his gun. The feel of it in his hand gave him comfort.

Merriam began to stir. He watched her writhe in the chair, her face a patchwork of alarm and confusion. Ray allowed her a few seconds to come to her senses, and then he demanded savagely, "Where the hell is the necklace?"

She stared at him in confusion, trying to decide if this situation was real or a nightmare.

"Your jewelry," he snapped impatiently. "Where is it?"

"I know you, don't I? I've seen you somewhere before?"

"We can discuss that later," he snapped. "Just tell me where the necklace is."

She shook her head. She was trembling visibly. "What necklace?"

"That vintage piece you wear for your boyfriend. You were wearing it not twenty minutes ago, dammit!"

"I met you in Don's Cookroom, didn't I? You're the salesman."

"We can discuss it later," he repeated. "Focus on the necklace. I need to know where it is."

Her eyes were on the gun in his hand, gawking at it like it was about to go off. Her concern made him lower the weapon.

"Who are you?" she demanded. "Why are you targeting me?"

He intended to tell her they would discuss it later, but she cut him off before he had a chance, saying, "You're not a burglar; you're a jewel thief. Aren't you? Is it just the necklace you want?"

He nodded. "Just the necklace. Let me have it, and I'll be on my way."

"I don't have it," she said defiantly. "My husband took it with him for safekeeping. It's just as well he did."

"Your husband! Is that what you call him?" Ray said jeeringly. "He's got quite the collection of wives, it seems. I watched him dash off in his Oldsmobile, and he definitely didn't take the necklace with him. It was around your neck when you stepped through that front door. Where did you stash it?"

The gun in his hand pointed at her again, and his finger pressed lightly on the trigger without him realizing it.

"Oh, God! This can't be happening," she moaned.

"Save it for your pastor," he snapped, his frustration growing.

"Please, let me go!" she urged.

"I can't leave without the necklace."

"Oh, that stupid necklace! I wish I had never seen it," she cried out bitterly. She looked hatefully at him, muttering, "You must have a screw loose. You break in here and assault me, all for some crummy piece of junk."

The gun in his hand waggled at her as he snarled, "If you believe it's a cheap bit of neck decoration, you would have handed it over already."

"What do you think I am, a European princess? You're willing to go to these despicable lengths to get your hands on it? What can be so important about it?"

"Tell me where you hid it, and I'll be out of your hair."

"Go to hell!" she screeched.

Ray's hand quivered, and the gun looked more menacing than ever. "Damn you," he muttered, lowering his weapon.

He took a threatening step forward. The temptation to strike her with the butt of the gun was overwhelming.

She gave a little moan, sensing he was about to hit her.

He turned his back on her sharply, not allowing her to see the blazing fury in his face. He was so tightly wound he feared he might be unable to control his temper. His thoughts drifted to the lonesome bottle of whiskey in his cabin; he had scarcely gotten to grips with it and abandoned it prematurely. The craving for another tumbler of its sweet liquid gripped his senses with severity.

He started pacing the room, trying to pull himself together. This line of questioning was getting him nowhere, but he didn't know what else to do. He told himself to bounce the obvious questions and see how she played them. Sometimes, people surprise you; occasionally, they drop their guard. Something about Merriam made him believe this wouldn't be the case. Her concentration was shot to pieces. Either that, or she was deliberately stalling him.

Ray kept pressing, convinced Sinclair didn't have the necklace. It was in the room somewhere, and Merriam would guide him to it.

"Where did Sinclair get it?" he asked, testing her reliability.

"A pawnbroker," she said with candor.

Her honesty revolted him. "Is that what Sinclair told you?"

She nodded.

"Which pawnbroker?"

"On Washington Street. Jenkins Jewelry and Loan."

Ray grabbed her hard by the hair, bringing her face close to his. "It's a lie! Do you really think he picked it up at that nickel and dime joint?"

She let out a despairing sob. Her head slumped forward when he let go of her hair, every ounce of fighting spirit deserting her.

His sense of compassion had evaporated with the hot air, and the tears didn't draw pity but hate. Far from the innocent damsel in distress, she was a gangster's moll; clearly, her partnership with Sinclair extended beyond the bedroom. She was part of his inner circle, a confidante, a business associate. As a cog in his racketeering operation, she knew the ins and outs of his organization, but Ray didn't care about the extent of her involvement. All he needed was that one simple piece of information.

His eyes darted wildly around the room, wondering where to focus his search. As upset and demoralized as Merriam seemed, he could tell she was determined to keep him from finding it. Whatever she told him would be contradictory and laced with lies, but he needed her to cooperate quickly. Their lives depended on it.

"Sinclair's not coming back tonight," he said, deciding to let her in on the unpleasant truth.

She looked up at him, disgust and anger written on her face. "He'll be here," she said with conviction.

"A sonofabitch named Carter has set his sights on rubbing him out and taking all that expensive loot your man keeps locked away in his safe room. He's a nasty piece of work is Carter. Someone tipped him off about the necklace. Perhaps someone whose nose got pushed out of joint by Sinclair or someone looking to stir up a hornet's nest. I guess it doesn't really matter who's responsible now. They've succeeded in pitching two criminal outfits against each other, landing us in trouble. It's doubtful you'll see Sinclair again. Carter will stop at nothing to get his hands on everything Sinclair owns, and when he's through with the reverend, he'll know everything there is to know about the smuggling operation you've got going. Naturally, he'll be along soon to see to you, too, sweetheart."

"I don't believe you," she said, though not with the same assuredness.

"Everything I've said is the absolute truth. We have eyes on Sinclair's church, and the latest news is that Carter and his gorillas have turned up, looking to take care of business. So far, they've gotten inside the building without a hitch. They're probably shooting their way through the church as we speak. Your lover is on his way there, about to run into a hot situation. What's he packing? A .38 Special and a crucifix? He'll need more than a peashooter and a prayer to come out of this scrape alive. Only divine intervention can save him now."

She didn't appear as crestfallen as he had hoped. "You seem to know everything."

"I like to keep myself well-informed."

"You *think* you know everything."

He shrugged. "I figure Sinclair might be able to hold them off for a while. You know what preachers are like. He'll talk their ears off, which buys us a bit of time, but he can't lie and bargain with them indefinitely. That big mouth of his will be sucking on the barrel of a gun soon enough. I'd say we have about another hour left, at most. Sinclair will soon be singing his life story to Carter's boys, and he'll get a bullet in his brain as a reward. Carter's gang won't stop until they've emptied out the church, processional cross, and candles as well. Then they'll come here to collect that necklace of yours."

"You don't know Arnold like I do," she said defiantly.

Ray stared at her coldly, annoyed by her naivety. The fingers on his left hand fiddled with the gun, the fingernails tapping against the gun barrel. Even if the crafty reverend could summon up an ingenious way to avoid meeting his maker, the chances of him returning to the motor court to fetch his mistress seemed even more unlikely.

Ray started to speak, intending to tell her that the reverend wasn't worth throwing her life away for, but then he decided against it. He'd known many young women like Merriam, infatuated fools with a misplaced sense of loyalty. She would hold her tongue, come what may, and protect her man, their jewels, their secrets, right up until her throat was cut. She apparently had atrocious taste in men and didn't want to believe that her lover was a pig, that he wouldn't shed a tear if someone hacked her open with a six-inch blade. She would go on loving him right into the next life, and Sinclair…well, if by some miracle he made it out of that church alive, he would probably move on to the next girl before her corpse was cold.

She would come to realize that Ray was her last hope, if she had any sense, and Ray had to believe that there was still sense left in her, even though she was hiding it well. Once Carter's gang arrived at their door, it would all be over for both of them. Ray knew he had to find a way to get it through to her that she could save her own neck by giving him the necklace.

"Enough with the stalling!" he growled. "We've wasted enough time already. Savage men are going to bust in here and start tearing up everything in this place. They'll begin with you, of course. Perhaps you'll be able to pull the wool over their eyes and keep that necklace all to yourself. Maybe you're tougher than you look."

"Let me disappear," she said, her voice barely audible.

He nodded distractedly. His eyes were dashing about the room, taking stock of everything, from the scuffed carpet and the dizzying wallflower wallpaper with its oppressively opaque background to the antiquated pieces of ramshackle furniture. Mentally, he was exploring every nook and crevice.

"Tell me where to look, Merriam," he implored.

She didn't reply, simply fidgeted in the chair, discreetly trying to free her wrists from the taut cloth that constrained her. In her struggle, she emitted a low, pained whimper that Ray hardly noticed.

He shoved the gun in his shoulder holster, wanting both hands free. Then he went straight to the highboy dresser and started pulling out the drawers and tossing them on the floor. His fast hands darted between the mattress and box spring in a frantic hunt. The sheets and pillows ended up on the floor, and the bed askew. He stomped across the room to the small wardrobe. The bottom section had a long drawer, but when he yanked it open, he found it was empty. The piece of furniture had four spindly legs, so he opened the doors with adequate care, then growled with irritation when he saw that the clothes rail held a set of wooden coat hangers but little else. Snatching Sinclair's suitcase off the luggage rack, he emptied everything onto the floor and hurriedly sifted through the garments. After examining the suitcase meticulously for hidden pockets, he angrily threw it across the room.

Carter and his gang couldn't have made more of a mess. It was all for nothing, though. Despite his thoroughness, his search came up empty.

He stomped toward Merriam, angry and frustrated, and in desperation, he threw himself on his knees before her, grabbing her chin and forcing her to look him in the eye. His handsome, russet brown eyes were the eyes of a lover, not a killer, although right now, they were cold and steely and devoid of charm.

"Tell me where it is," he said brusquely. "Christ! Tell me where to look. Be sensible, dammit!"

Her beautiful, pale blue eyes hardened, and then, all of a sudden, she spat at him.

He swore and scrambled to his feet. The palm of his hand caught her roughly on the cheek, knocking the breath out of her. His hand returned, eager to administer more retribution, but he managed to control his temper just in time.

"I should walk out of here, leave you trussed up in that chair," he muttered angrily. "I'm sure Carter's pack of savages would love to find a girl like you in this compromising position." He gave her a malicious smile, but the desperation in his eyes told her to dismiss this as an empty threat.

His hands twitched wildly, his aggravation building. He was painfully aware of the time he had squandered, ransacking the room and needlessly bruising Merriam's face. He was filled with an intoxicating desire to pound down the claustrophobic walls. With a grimace, he thought back to an earlier conversation with Walter. The old man believed that dealing with the gentler sex was child's play. "Play to their vanity and exert your physical dominance, Ray, when necessary," he had advised. *Child's play, indeed!* Obviously, Walter had little dealings with women, as nothing is straightforward when a dame is involved.

Of course, to a rich, pampered old man, everything seems easy, thought Ray. All he has to do is dial a telephone number and issue an order. He knows nothing of hard work. It's somebody else that does the heavy lifting.

"You're a pathetic dog," Merriam declared, bringing him out of his reverie. "You enjoy hurting people, especially women."

"You know what *I* think?"

"Nobody cares what *you* think."

"I'll tell you anyway. I think you're deliberately trying to provoke me. You want me to smack you so hard that you'll pass out from the pain. You think that if you can keep the violence going, you'll buy yourself time. You truly believe that your

Arnold will make it back here tonight. You still have hope you'll be rescued."

She said nothing, just glowered at him.

"When Carter arrives, you'll wish you'd listened to me. I'm not like him, if that's what you're thinking. If I wanted to kill you, I'd have made your death quick and painless. I'm not the type who's naturally drawn to violence."

"You're a sadistic pig!" she countered.

"Not true," he growled, but there was doubt in his voice.

The jobs Walter assigned him required him to perform a wide range of unpleasant tasks. Though his crimes were many, murder was not among them, and he did not derive pleasure from torture, no matter how deplorable the victim. Tough as he appeared on the outside, Ray was no hard case. He was more humane than most, or so he liked to think. When faced with the difficult task of extracting information from an unwilling subject, many might let their frustrations get the better of them. *The aptitude for violence is in everyone*, Ray maintained. And yet, he liked to think of himself as restrained, persuasive, and levelheaded. Wasn't the reason Walter placed so much faith in him because he valued his level of restraint?

Before tonight, Ray considered the menacing knife Len had supplied him with to be a prop rather than a genuine weapon. It was to be a false threat, a means of intimidation. Now, he viewed it differently. Right now, he saw it as a precious necessity.

With time and optimism rapidly expiring, his panicky hand reached into his pocket, clasping the switchblade with fierce urgency. It was time for the knife to make an impression, an opportunity for the nasty little blade to be put to good use. Prop or not, one way or another, that shiv would serve to make Merriam spill everything she knew about the necklace.

Thirteen

Ray's hand emerged from his pocket, gripping the switchblade. His thumb drifted naturally to the button on the handle, and with a faint *click*, a mean-looking six-inch blade sprang out.

Merriam jerked in her seat at the sight of the shiv.

"Let's hear more about the necklace," he said irritably, angling the knifepoint toward her face. "Is it worth dying for?"

"Oh, God!" she said with a shudder.

He waggled the blade impatiently, demanding an answer.

She swallowed nervously and focused on his shirt sleeve, trying not to acknowledge the blade. Its presence brought a tang of faintness to her, a wave of nausea to overcome.

Ray noticed her discomfort and saw that there were tiny beads of sweat glistening on her forehead. Her evident anxiety brought him solace. He knew she was a tough broad. There was nothing soft about her, in fact. She was a woman with pluck, who wore about ten layers of armor at all times, but he sensed that right now, she might be ready to divulge information with perhaps a whiff of honesty.

"There's something you ought to know about the necklace," she gingerly explained, intriguing him. "It looks very fancy, and it's true I'm loath to part with it."

She paused, letting the seconds drag out. It was an inordinate pause, and he found it deeply irritating. He nodded and waggled the blade, desperate for her to go on.

"But honestly, I highly doubt it's as valuable as you believe. Arnold picked it up during his missionary work in India. I suspect it's practically worthless."

"More lies," said Ray crossly.

He made his way to the telephone on the side table, stomping across the room petulantly. His fingers jabbed at the numbers with aggression, the dial seeming to take an age to rotate back to the rest position. There was an unexpectedly long wait before Walter picked up the call.

"It's Ray. I'm calling from Merriam's cabin. Any new developments?"

"Do you have the necklace?" asked the old man tetchily.

"Not yet. I need more time."

"Where's Merriam? Is she dead?"

"No, she's here. She's tied up."

A noise in the background distracted Ray, and then two thin streaks of light flickered across the curtain. They were gone in an instant.

"Hold on. I think a car has turned up," Ray said, putting the receiver down on the table.

He went to the window and peered out, expecting to see a car, but it was quiet out front. He counted the vehicles in the parking lot to make sure there were no new arrivals.

"Strange," he muttered, returning to the telephone.

"What's wrong?" asked Walter.

"I thought I heard a car, but I was mistaken. Might have been a motorist using the parking lot to turn around in."

"Ray, you should hurry up and find that necklace."

Ray said, full of bitterness, "What do you think I'm doing? House cleaning? You think this is easy?"

"Of course not. I knew it would be a bit of a challenge, but I expected you'd have it by now. I don't know what's happening there, but you must find it quickly and get out. I have a bad feeling about this."

"Yes, yes, I'm working on it!" Shards of frustration cleaved through his words. He didn't want to admit that his guileless efforts had brought no reward and simply cost him precious time. He knew he was up against the clock, and this pointless conversation with Walter wasn't helping matters. "You have anything for me, Walter? What's the latest news from the church?"

"My man hasn't got back to me. He's not answering his telephone."

Ray looked at Merriam to make sure she was still securely bound and seated in the chair. "Okay. Call me when you hear something."

He read out the telephone number to Walter and then rang off.

When Ray looked at Merriam, he saw her fidgeting frantically in her seat, trying to loosen the knots binding her wrists. The way she was squirming, he reckoned she must be making good progress.

"It might be wise to cut your throat," he said soberly. "This cabin isn't so big. If I tear the place up good, I'll find the necklace soon enough."

She continued to writhe in her seat. The way she was working her hips made him nervous. The knots were loose; she would be out of the chair in no time. She had caused him sufficient problems earlier, so the thought of her getting free of her restraints made him nervous.

He scurried across the room and let the tip of his blade pass lightly across her throat. He was seeking the most efficient point to penetrate the larynx.

"Wait!" she pleaded.

"I'm out of time," he said, sounding apologetic.

She cried out in despair when the cold blade dug into her flesh, causing a tiny bead of blood to appear. "Stop! I'll tell you everything."

He kept the point of the blade pressed against her neck, but not hard enough for it to do significant harm. "You have two minutes to talk. Just two, that's all. Then I make a little incision right here." He wriggled the blade, scratching her skin with the knifepoint. "After that, I plan to drive the whole damn blade into your goddamn throat."

She swallowed nervously. The color had drained from her face, and she felt very weak. The broken look in her eyes was a welcome sight. Ray wished he had taken the knife to her skin much earlier.

"It's not what you think. It's a replica," she revealed. "Arnold doesn't have the real Hessman's Necklace."

Her use of the man's name startled Ray. "You know about Hessman? You know the history of the necklace?"

"Some of it. I know that Herman Hessman found it in 1928 and sold it to the Jamaican government for one hundred and thirty thousand dollars. But did you know he was also the one who later stole it?"

Ray waggled the knife, urging her to go on.

"Before he sold it to the government, he had two replicas made. When it was housed in the national museum, he paid a curator to switch the original with the replica. The theft wasn't noticed until almost twenty years later. It was only when a royal visit from the Queen of England was being arranged that the discovery was made."

Ray chewed his lip, wondering if he should believe her or if this was another of her lies. "Why would Hessman make two replicas?"

"Unfortunately, I don't have the answer to that mystery. I do have some theories, though." She paused, fidgeting in her seat. "Would you mind untying my wrists? The nylon is cutting off the circulation, and I can no longer feel my fingers."

"I can't do that," he said, indifferent to the pained look on her face.

He had come to realize that he was dealing with a very sly creature. She had told him all sorts of tales tonight, denying all knowledge of the necklace and then trying to hoodwink him that it was of Indian origin. Now, she claimed it was counterfeit. She seemed to know so much about the ornament that Ray wondered if her last admission was close to the truth.

He glanced at his watch once more and moaned in dismay. Precious minutes kept slipping away, words getting him nowhere.

"Don't you want to hear my theories? Aren't you interested?"

"Of course," he said with a weary sigh. "But I doubt there's time."

"You said you wanted to hear more about the necklace."

"I know."

"Doesn't Hessman interest you? Isn't it intriguing?"

"Yes, yes. It's all very fascinating, isn't it? But hell, I'm still no closer to finding the damn thing."

The telephone suddenly came to life, startling them both. Ray hurried to the side table and snatched up the receiver. Walter was on the line, yelling in his ear, "Get the hell out of there! Now!"

Ray fumbled the receiver, dropping the knife and almost knocking the telephone off the table. "I don't have the necklace yet," he told Walter. "I'm not closer to finding it. I need more time. What's the situation? How long do I have?"

"Günter sold me out. He double-crossed me, Ray. Get out of there!"

Ray rested the receiver on the table and dashed to the window. He pulled back the curtain and stared out at the parking lot. No new cars had arrived, leading him to believe he must still have time to search for the necklace.

He wrestled with the curtain, trying to put it back into position, wanting to shield his activities from prying eyes. More seconds trailed way as he strolled back to the table and picked up the receiver. "No one is around outside. All is safe at the moment," he told Walter. "Is Carter's gang on their way here?"

"Carter's dead."

"Dead?" Ray said incredulously. He gripped the telephone receiver tightly, managing to control a slight tremor. "What happened?"

"There was a gunfight at the church. Carter and his men are all dead."

"All of them?"

"Get out of there, Ray. He's coming for you!"

"Who's coming for me?"

He didn't hear the answer to his question. A split second later, the motel door was kicked open with violent force. The telephone receiver jumped from Ray's hand and clonked against the table.

The roar of a big Colt Python revolver reverberated across the room, and Ray was projected backward, banging into the coffee table and an armchair and collapsing onto the floor. A second bullet crashed into the upturned coffee table, spraying shards of glass across the room.

Ray growled and writhed in pain on the floor, clutching his left shoulder where a bullet had clipped him, rendering his arm useless. He heard the soft thud of footsteps, and straightaway, he scrambled across the carpet and reached for the knife that was a few feet away.

The Colt roared again, making Ray flatten himself against the floor. The bullet zipped over his head and slammed into the wall.

Ray drew himself to his knees and pounced on the switchblade, getting his fingers on the handle. A hulking shadow loomed over him as he twisted around and flung the knife blindly at the figure bearing down on him. He was ambidextrous, and his left arm was the weaker of the two, but his throw was decent.

There was a soft *thunk* as the blade struck the thick, wooden crucifix peeping out of the shooter's jacket pocket. Ray stared in anguish at the knife protruding ineffectually from the sturdy hunk of wood.

Reverend Sinclair examined the crucifix incredulously, not

quite believing his eyes. Then he threw the heavy cross aside and leveled his gun at Ray. "Eat on this, rat-face," he snarled.

Ray sprang to his feet and lunged for Sinclair, but the pastor's finger closed on the trigger before he had a chance.

A bullet tore into Ray's chest at close range, thrusting his body against the wall with sickening force. His inert body then thudded to the ground uncouthly, his head lolling to one side, propped up awkwardly against the baseboard.

Merriam's hysterical voice in the background jolted his eyes open. He squinted at Sinclair, watching the man crouch down and yank the switchblade out of the crucifix.

"I'm so sorry, darling," said Sinclair, hurrying across the room to Merriam. "I got here as fast as possible. I should never have left you here alone."

He knelt beside her and used the switchblade to cut through the nylon fabric binding her wrists and ankles.

"Thank God I'm not too late. What did that bastard do to you?"

"I'm okay, Arnold. I'm okay," she said between sobs.

Ray's fading eyes watched the reverend gently cradle Merriam in his arms, kissing her passionately and whispering words of comfort in her ear.

As the life spilled out of Ray, forming a bloody pool on the carpet, he listened to the sounds of Merriam's joyful weeping, and he thought about how wrong he had been about the reverend. Crooked, murderous swine that he was, Sinclair was a dutiful, courageous lover who had come back to rescue his sweetheart. Merriam had been right to put so much stock in him returning for her. They were well suited.

Ray's eyes drifted upward, circling the ceiling, trying desperately to fix his gaze on something. He was intensely weak and wooly-eyed and felt an overwhelming desire to close his eyes and let sleep take hold.

That's when he noticed the ceiling fan. It was oddly adorned and quite beautiful, yet something seemed out of place. His gaze hardened as he stared at the hub-mounted rotating paddles. Something was insecurely looped around the blades, a glittery metallic string that had no right being there and that looked as if it might come loose at any moment.

Ray was suddenly filled with awed disbelief.

Merriam drew the reverend's attention to the fan, and when Sinclair looked up, squinting at the bizarre embellishment, he started to chuckle.

"What a place to put your jewelry, darling. I trust you didn't throw it up there. It's worth a lot of money, you know."

"Yes. People are willing to kill for it," she murmured.

Ray stared long and hard at the exquisite emerald–studded objet d'art, glowing magnificently. Then, all comprehension was gone from his handsome, russet brown eyes, and all that remained was an empty, glassy stare.

Afterword

Hessman's Necklace began as a short story intended for *Alfred Hitchcock Magazine*. It was written in 2016, and it took exactly eleven months for the editors to retrieve it from their mammoth slush pile, carefully deliberate over its merits, and then grudgingly send a form rejection.

I wasn't discouraged, deciding to expand the story into a novelette and place it with *Black Mask*. That magazine, launched in 1920, lasted for decades, featuring stories by the likes of Dashiell Hammett, Raymond Chandler, Erle Stanley Gardner, Cornell Woolrich, and John D. MacDonald. It ceased publication in 1951, and attempts to revive it in the 1970s and 80s were unsuccessful. However, Steeger Properties acquired it in 2016 and relaunched it as an online magazine.

Turning the story into a novelette was a relatively speedy, enjoyable challenge, and the finished product felt like a great fit for the magazine. It was subsequently accepted for publication in January 2018 with the online incarnation of *Black Mask*. As a fan, it was a proud moment. However, I couldn't sign the contract as I couldn't bear letting go of it. I hoped to publish the piece in a story collection someday or expand it into a novella, but the contract didn't allow me to do that, and it was non-negotiable.

I cast the novelette aside to work on other things, but every year or so, I found myself trying to rework the story into something resembling a novel. Every effort to expand it necessitated extensive character rewrites, and it became an infuriating jumble of half-written chapters. Scenes didn't go anywhere, and Merriam, the heart of the story, was tough to track down. I just couldn't picture her. She was as enigmatic as the reverend.

It took six years before I felt I could declare it finally done. The problem was that, as a novella, there wasn't much of a market for it. It was either too long or too short. I decided it would find a more suitable home as part of a story collection, but as I pitched the project to publishers, it quickly became apparent that it was a mistake. It would have worked better as a novelette. In its present form, it swamped the other pieces.

There was only one recourse: make it into a novel and let it stand on its own.

I've come to believe that writing something new is easier than editing past work. Lately, I've gotten into the habit of writing a story or a novelette from scratch in one day and refining it over a week. *Hessman's Necklace*, on the other hand, has been a mammoth, hair-pulling experience spanning eight years. At times, the end never felt within reach, which is funny, considering that the beginning, the ending, and all the bits in the middle have been there all along.

Surprisingly, it's hard to mark a manuscript as finished and send it off without any intention of adding a final sentence. This time, with this story, I'm happy to declare there's nothing more I have to say. Farewell, Merriam, and enjoy the necklace.

About the Author

Nicholas Litchfield is the author of the novels *When The Actor Inspired Chaos and Bloodshed* and *Swampjack Virus* and editor of twelve literary anthologies. His stories, essays, and book reviews appear in *BULL*, *Colorado Review*, *Daily Press*, *Shotgun Honey*, *The MacGuffin*, *The Virginian-Pilot*, *Washington Square Review*, and elsewhere. He has contributed introductions to numerous books, including twenty-two Stark House Press reprints of long-forgotten noir and mystery novels. Formerly a book critic for the *Lancashire Post*, syndicated to twenty-five newspapers across the U.K., he now writes for *Publishers Weekly*. You can find him online at nicholaslitchfield.com or Twitter: @NLitchfield.

WHEN THE ACTOR INSPIRED CHAOS AND BLOODSHED

by NICHOLAS LITCHFIELD

"Litchfield's entertaining and gritty novel reads like a 1970s car chase shot with a handheld camera, full of jolts and scrapes and Technicolor chaos."
—ADAM BERLIN, author of *Belmondo Style*

"A refreshingly different take on international thrillers. Litchfield makes the most of his South American setting in this cinematic page-turner that will keep you engrossed to the very end."
—TIMOTHY J. LOCKHART, author of *Smith* and *Pirates*

"Fast-paced, violent, and horrifying. It's a made-for-Hollywood novel that testifies to the author's ability to keep readers on the edge of their seats. I couldn't put it down."
—MARY DONALDSON-EVANS, author of *Madame Bovary at the Movies*

"Litchfield holds nothing back in this edgy romp... Ceaseless action and witty dialogue whip the reader through Dominic's crazy life at a cyclone pace in this unrelenting peak into filmmaking hell."
—LINDA BOROFF, screenwriter of *Murder in Fashion*

"A cinematic page-turner about Hollywood gone by, movie-making, and a throwback to a golden age of hard-boiled stories of noir and shadows, questionable morals, devious sins, and the unforgettable characters that made that world their own."
—CHRISTOPHER COSMOS, bestselling author of *Once We Were Here*

"Take ambition, greed, and a dash of corruption and mix them thoroughly on a movie set. Place it in a hot climate until boiling, and you will have the recipe for Nicholas Litchfield's entertaining novel."
—SHELDON RUSSELL, author of the Hook Runyan Mystery Series

To order, visit www.lowestoftchronicle.com

The Vicarious Traveler

Edited by NICHOLAS LITCHFIELD
Foreword by Michael C. Keith

"I savored every locale. From the richly drawn desolation of the Texas panhandle in Sharon Frame Gay's "Song of the Highway" to the lush, bird-teeming lawns of "The Buzzing" by Philip Barbara; from the American nostalgia of "Mr. O'Brien's Last Soliloquy" by Robert Garner McBrearty to the Turkish apple orchard of Dave Gregory, this collection abounds with amazing language, arresting insight, and sharply drawn landscapes."
—LINDA BOROFF, screenwriter of *Murder in Fashion*

"Charm, a love of travel, often sly humor, and a clear reverence of story make up the backbone of *Lowestoft Chronicle*."
—KEITH ROSSON, acclaimed author of *Fever House* and *Smoke City*

"*The Vicarious Traveler* is a welcome travel-themed anthology that has something for everyone—adventure, crime, and humor all served up in sparkling prose and poetry."
—TIMOTHY J. LOCKHART, acclaimed author of *Smith*

An Adventurous Spirit

Edited by NICHOLAS LITCHFIELD
Foreword by James B. Nicola

"An amusing anthology of writing about travel. Among the many standout works is Tim Frank's "Three Strikes," whose premise is inventively and uncomfortably dark, and readers will savor its devilish twist. Meanwhile, poems such as "Woman With the Red Carry-On" are drolly perceptive."
—KIRKUS REVIEWS

"This anthology is a wideranging showcase of *Lowestoft Chronicle*'s writers, and the reader cannot help but be changed by this collective force."
—CAT DIXON, *The Good Life Review* Poetry Editor

"*An Adventurous Spirit* moves deftly, displays a remarkable range, and reminds us why we crave travel literature. Read and enjoy!"
—CHARLES HOLDEFER, author of *The Contractor*

"A treasure trove of excellent writing. This volume lives up to its claim of spirited adventure... The poetry also is remarkable. This book is a great find."
—JULIA MCMICHAEL, *Seattle Book Review*

Intrepid Travelers

A Place to Pause

Edited by NICHOLAS LITCHFIELD
Foreword by Mary Donaldson-Evans

To order, visit www.lowestoftchronicle.com

www.ingramcontent.com/pod-product-compliance
Lightning Source LLC
Chambersburg PA
CBHW020338260626
47156CB00004B/1586